HISTORIES OF
THE DEAD

AND OTHER STORIES

MATH BIRD

MCSNOWELL BOOKS

A McSnowel Book

First published by All Due Respect Books, 2018
This edition published by McSnowell Books, 2021

For Betty and Dai.
Two little birds who will be forever loved and remembered.

CONTENTS

HISTORIES OF THE DEAD

The realisation Stevey is dead returns to me in flashes. Like a rotten tooth, it suddenly strikes a nerve and throbs inside me. It's nothing anyone says that brings it all back. It's these old Beatles songs he used to love. They keep playing them on the radio.

They found Stevey's body down the Level, a hilly stretch of grassland where they once mined for lead. His clothes soaked in blood, or so everyone said, his face barely recognisable.

Anyone who knew Stevey guessed that Wayne Myatt had something to do with it. But anybody who knows Wayne Myatt keeps such notions left unsaid.

'Are you gonna change that tyre, Jase,' old Berry shouts, 'or gawp at it all day?'

'Sorry,' I say, and turn off the radio.

Berry stands in front of me, says I can leave early. He strokes his beard, gives me that look of his. It's as though he can read my mind, see right through me.

'How's that girl of yours?' he asks. 'The pretty one with dark hair.'

'Tina?'

Berry nods.

'She's okay, I suppose. But she's not my girl. We split up years ago.'

'You should go and see her, Jase, might even cheer you up.'

I walk over to the sink and scrub the oil from my hands. 'How come you're suddenly interested in my love life?'

Berry pretends not to hear. But he's fooling no one. That old man spends half his life worrying about me. It's not as though he's got no one else to care about. He has a daughter and a son.

I wipe my hands down my face, picturing Tina as a fresh breeze tingles across my skin.

'My love life,' I say, stepping back into the workshop.

'What about it?'

'Why you so interested?'

'I couldn't care less, just thought it'd be a good idea if you were distracted.'

'Why's that?'

'All this business with Stevey. I know you boys were close, but best let the police handle it.'

'Jesus, Berry. What do you think I'm gonna do?'

'I don't know. That's what concerns me. You see what you're like with that temper of yours.'

'Used to be, I haven't had a drink in ages.'

Berry glances at the floor. 'Stevey hasn't been right in the head for years, not since his accident. I'm not saying the lad deserved it. But you know better than anyone about the things that boy got up to.'

. . .

As I DRIVE AWAY from Berry's garage, I see Jordy on the Well Hill. He's dressed in black; a crop of grey curls covers his head. My short, stocky friend is unmistakable.

I pull up alongside him, wind down the window. 'Where you off?' I ask, already knowing the answer.

Jordy grins. 'Down the valley for a smoke.'

'Hop in, I'll take you down the hill.'

I drive past the Holy Well of St. Winefride's. It's over eight hundred years old, and they still come here to redeem themselves. I tried that once. Drunk as hell, jumped right into the pool. Even begged God for forgiveness. He didn't answer me, though. No. All he gave me was a cold.

I park up by the Well's entrance. 'How far are you going?' I ask.

Jordy shrugs. 'Probably to the Flour Mill Pool.'

I mull it over. 'You know Jordy, I haven't been there for years, think I'll join you.'

Just under two miles long, the Greenfield Valley was prosperous in its day. Shamefully, that's all I know. Jordy's the man with the degree. He knows its history.

We follow the path through the woods. 'When was that built?' I ask, pointing to the ruins of an old factory.

Jordy shrugs. 'Don't know the exact date, probably mid to late eighteenth century.'

'What did it make?'

'Stuff from copper, you know, wire and bolts.'

We walk the rest of the way in silence. And I try to imagine how this place used to look. But all I can see are the ghosts. I catch glimpses of them, two teenage boys, chasing each other through the trees.

Finally, we reach the pool. The swans are out, gliding across the water. We hunker down among the reeds and

Jordy lights up a joint. He draws on it three times, then offers me a toke.

'Just a small one,' I say and make some excuse about driving. I take a deep drag, holding the smoke inside my chest.

Jordy shakes his head. 'Jesus,' he whispers, 'poor old Stevey.'

I nod, keeping my eyes closed while I exhale.

'What did this pool used to be?' I say, desperate to change the subject.

'A reservoir, to power the old mill.'

'Doesn't seem possible.'

'Well, it was. That old spring pumped four thousand gallons of water a minute.'

I stare at him for a moment. 'This place must have been something.'

Jordy shrugs. 'I suppose if you believe everything you read in books.'

'What do you mean?'

'We only get to see one side of it. I bet, for most, this was just a place they worked, another shitty job.'

'But ten times worse, I bet.'

Jordy nods. 'Too right, especially for those poor souls in the factory. Nah, we'll never know the real story.'

'What makes you so sure?'

Jordy smiles. 'Because my friend, history's never written by the dead.'

JORDY'S WORDS niggle me all day, lingering like a stale taste in the mouth. I don't know if the notion's his, but it sure as hell applies to Stevey.

Like me, Jordy was born on the Moor Estate. He's lived

nowhere else. He even did his degree in Liverpool, took the train there every day.

This estate was so much better when we were kids, full of families like Jordy's and my own. People like my mum and dad, rough as they come, yet generous and hard working.

Of course, we had the occasional interlopers: an Irish bachelor, a blonde-haired family of Rhodesians. Mostly they were transients, people waiting to get better housing and moving the moment they did.

Old Berry blames immigration for the estate's decline. But like most people in this town, he aims his arrows at the easiest targets. If you ask me, most of the trouble comes from across the river, the dealers and the wannabe-gangsters, scum like Wayne Myatt, feeding on the rot within.

THE HOUSE FEELS quiet when I get in. The slow tick of the clock stresses the silence. Mum left me the place in her will. She bought it in the late 80s, just after Dad passed away. It's the only thing Maggie Thatcher's Britain ever gave us, the chance to own a council house, a pauper's right to buy.

I've changed the place over the years. Something I regret now. Don't get me wrong, the house is still full of memories. I've kept all the photographs. Dad's boxing trophies. Mum's porcelain figurines.

But sometimes it's not enough, especially when the nights are long. Sometimes I don't know what to do with myself. I just sit here, regretting the past, as me and this house grow older.

. . .

MYATT PLAYS his music just after eight. It's the same old shit, reverberating bass pumping like a giant heart.

I watch him from the landing, peering through the chink in the curtains.

Myatt's sitting outside, a can of beer in his hand, watching the world from his sofa. His cronies stand around him. Most of them are kids, hanging on his every word. He points his finger as he speaks, and occasionally he'll stand and swing a punch at the air. The boys step aside when he does this, some of them laugh nervously, while others just look away. Every pair of eyes seems frightened, though. I don't know why. The only advantage he has is his height. The rest of him is just skin and bone. He looks a mess if you ask me. That grey hooded tracksuit he always wears draped over him like an old rag.

I must have pushed my face out too far because Myatt stops talking and looks up at me. Usually I look away, but tonight I hold his stare with my own. He grins, gives me the finger. Years ago, I'd have been straight out there. But that's history now. Instead, I turn around and walk away.

IT'S the banging on the front door that wakes me, saves me, in fact, rescues me from a bad dream.

'I'm coming now,' I shout, the persistent banging getting on my nerves.

When I open the front door, Tina storms right in. She heads to the living room, sits down on the sofa. I follow her inside and throw back the curtains, my eyes squinting in the morning light.

I switch on the gas fire, sit in the chair opposite. Tina stares ahead, her body trembling.

'What's wrong?' I ask.

She breathes deeply, closes her eyes for a moment. 'It's Ben. That boy will be the death of me.'

'Why? What's he done?'

She glances at the window. 'He's hanging around with that gobshite.'

'Myatt?'

Tina nods. 'Ben hasn't been home since Thursday.'

'I suppose he's old enough to do what he wants.'

Tina glares at me. 'He's only sixteen, Jase. He needs to do what I say.'

I consider myself told, and motion towards my cigarettes. Tina grabs the pack from the sofa and slings it onto my lap. I pop one in my mouth, catching her perfume as she hands me my lighter. She hasn't changed much. She still wears her hair in a ponytail, its dark glossiness highlighting the smoothness of her skin.

I blow the smoke away from her. 'Don't take this the wrong way, Tina. But what do you expect from me?'

'Go and fetch him.'

'Why?'

She gives me that look of hers. 'You know what Myatt's like, look what happened to Stevey.'

AFTER A QUICK SWILL, I make my way across the street. Tina walks behind me, keeping her distance.

Myatt's garden is a war zone. Bin bags line the path, the grass strewn with cans.

A damp smell taints the air, and I wonder what I'm doing knocking on a killer's door.

Myatt leans out of his bedroom window, reminding me how ugly he is, pale, spotty, eyes still half shut. 'What d'you want, man? It's half nine in the morning.'

He tells me the time as though I'm unaware of it. Then he stares at me. His eyes widen when I take no heed of his threat.

'Is Ben there?' I ask.

'Ben who?'

'Ben Carlyle,' Tina shouts from behind me.

Myatt scans her figure. 'Never heard of 'im, love. Now jog on.' He slams the window shut.

Tina hammers against the door until I grab her arm and make her stand behind me. I hear Myatt stomping down the stairs. His blurred, pale shape hovers behind the frosted glass. He opens the door. He's wearing a pair of grey joggers and is naked from the waist up. I stare at his homemade tattoos, which remind me of an infant's scrawl. One of them spells MUM, and for a moment I pity the poor woman who conceived him.

Myatt drops his arms to his sides, sticks his chest out. 'Which part of that didn't you understand? On your way, don't make me tell ya again.'

'I want to see my son,' Tina says. 'I heard he was staying with you.'

Myatt takes a deep breath, his pig-like lashes flickering as he lets the air out. He looks over his shoulder down the hallway. 'Cody,' he shouts, 'fetch me that bat.'

A shaven-headed youth swaggers out of the kitchen, a baseball bat in his hand, its notched barrel resting on his bony shoulder. As he hands the bat over to Myatt, three more boys shuffle into the hall. One of them is Ben, yawning, his puffy eyes almost shut.

'Where the hell have you been?' Tina shouts, bringing her son to his senses.

'Out,' Ben says, the attitude in his voice encouraged by his friends' laughter.

Myatt looks at him. 'Ben? I thought your name was Spider.'

Ben blushes, then stares down at the carpet.

'Mummy wants you home, Ben,' Myatt says. 'But nobody's forcing ya to go.'

Tina steps forward. 'It's nothing to do with you. This is between my son and me.'

Myatt pushes his face out, his forehead almost touching the bridge of Tina's nose.

I throw Ben a look, and he's savvy enough to get my meaning. He squeezes through a gap. Shakes his head at Tina and follows her up the path.

'Run along home then,' Myatt shouts. 'Do what Mummy tells ya.'

As I'm about to turn round, Myatt grips the bat and prods me in the chest. 'I'll see you again. I'll teach ya to come knocking on my door.'

I notice the stains on the bat, wondering if it's Stevey's blood. Then my eyes fix on Myatt's, and I don't know what he sees in them, but they sure as hell shut him up.

I GET LOST in those listless hours of a Sunday afternoon. I pace the room, trying not to think about Stevey.

I flick through one of Mum's old paperbacks. But I've never had the head for reading. Just as I breathe out the deepest sigh I can manage, someone knocks on the door. I peer through the curtains and to my surprise I see Ben. He's got his hands in his pockets. His expression tells the world this is the last place he wants to be.

When I open the door, Ben steps back. 'All right,' he grunts. 'Mum wants you to come for lunch.'

'When?'

'Now, I suppose.'

'Okay. Tell her I'll be there soon.'

I SHOULD BRING a bottle of wine, but someone might see me. Then the gossip will run rife, spreading like a valley fire, and before I know it, everyone will say that Jase is back on the drink. Instead, I buy some flowers, reckoning it's the next best thing.

When I arrive at Tina's, she opens the front door before I even have time to knock.

'Where've you been?' she says. 'I sent Ben around half an hour ago.'

'Sorry. I thought I'd try to look presentable.'

She eyes me up and down. 'You'll do, I suppose, which is more than I can say for those flowers.'

'The woman in the garage picked them. She told me they were fresh from this morning.'

Tina laughs. 'Fresh from where exactly, the garage bin or the skip?'

She takes the flowers from my hand, and I follow her into the house. She nods towards the dining room. 'Ben's in there. Dinner will be ready in a bit.'

AFTER DINNER, Ben slopes off to play his X-Box while Tina and I chat on the sofa.

'You look exhausted, Jase,' she says.

I slap my hands down onto my stomach. 'That's your fault, fattening me up with all that meat and veg.'

She smiles, but only for a moment. 'Seriously, Jase, you need to relax. Stop blaming yourself. I've a bottle of wine in the fridge.'

'No thanks. I've barely touched a drop since the accident.'

'That was sixteen years ago. It wasn't your fault. You were just boys, drunk, messing around.'

'I know, but I should've...'

'Should've what?'

'Kept an eye on him, maybe things would have turned out different.'

Tina moves closer, 'The Stevey that died wasn't the Stevey we knew. That was someone else. He was like a child. It's not your fault, Jase. His family should've taken better care of him.'

'Perhaps. All I know is that he didn't deserve it.'

Tina rubs my arm, then brushes her thigh against my own. She massages my shoulder, her warm breath breezing across my skin. Just as we're about to kiss, I pull my head back. 'Sorry, I'm not trying to mess you about. It's too soon, you know, after Stevey.'

She nods and we slump back into the sofa. We sit quietly for a while. I say, 'Ben was quiet during lunch.'

Tina looks up at the ceiling. 'That was Ben being sociable. You should see him on a bad day.'

'How long has he been friendly with Myatt?'

'A couple of weeks, he says, but it's more like a few months.'

'Has he said anything?'

'What about?'

'Stevey.'

Tina shakes her head. 'He used to go on about him all the time. Said he felt sorry for him. That Myatt was always sending Stevey on errands, knocking him around. But he hasn't mentioned Stevey for weeks. Not since...'

'Has he mentioned the police?'

Tina chews her lip. 'No, only that they took Myatt in for questioning. They've got nothing on him. Those boys think the sun shines out of his arse. He's got a hundred alibis. I'm worried sick about Ben, Jase. Do you think he can spend some time with you?'

'In the garage?'

'Just for a few days. You don't have to pay him or anything. It'll just give him something to do.'

WHEN I GET TO WORK, Berry has already opened up. He nods at me. The best you can expect on a Monday morning. Then I notice Ben loitering by the window.

'Berry, this is Ben,' I say.

Berry nods. 'So I believe. Apparently, he's going to be helping us.' Berry throws me a look that says you might have asked me.

Ben spends the first hour looking for striped paint and left-handed screwdrivers. It doesn't take him long to click, and by lunchtime the jokes are wearing thin. He laughs it off, though. He even gives Berry one of his sandwiches.

'Do you have a girlfriend, Ben?' Berry asks, revealing a mouthful of egg and cress.

Ben's ears and neck turn red. 'Nah, that's not for me.'

Berry holds the sandwich in front of his mouth. 'Really, and why's that then?'

Ben looks him in the eye. 'Because these days I'm into fighting.'

'Well, I'm sorry to hear that, Ben.'

'Why?'

Berry sighs, 'Because you've just told the world you're a prick.'

I look at Ben and shake my head, trying to reassure him.

'Berry speaks as he finds. Over the years, I've learned to take no notice.'

Berry glares at me, then climbs back into the pit.

Ben's face stays red. But from the look in his eyes, it's more from the embarrassment than anything Berry said.

'Berry's right, though,' I say. 'Fighting for the sake of it, you know yourself that's just for dicks.'

Ben smiles, opens his mouth as if he's about to say something.

'Listen,' I say. 'That stuff with Myatt, yesterday. Your mum was worried sick.'

'I know, but she didn't have to embarrass me.'

'Embarrass you in front of who? Those idiots?'

'They're my mates.'

'What about Myatt? Is he your mate, too?'

'Myatt's cool. He's all right when you get to know him.'

'Yeah, right. It's probably all those years he spent in charm school.'

Ben laughs, and for a moment he reminds me of Stevey.

I throw him a rag. 'Let's wipe this one down,' I say, and he follows me to a Ford Fiesta.

'What do you get up to then, with these so-called mates of yours?'

'Not much, you know, this and that.'

'Seems vague if you ask me, you sound like a man with a secret.'

'What's that supposed to mean? What's Mum been telling you?'

'Nothing, I've got eyes in my head to see.'

'See what exactly?'

I wipe the fender. 'I see you young lads, dicking about, doing all of Myatt's dealing.'

Ben clenches the rag in his fist. 'You shouldn't say things like that. You don't want Myatt to hear you.'

'And why's that?'

'He's off his head, Jase. He'll kill you, especially if he loses his temper.'

'Is that what happened to Stevey?'

Ben drops the rag onto the floor. 'Listen, I need to go.'

I grab his arm. 'Don't go just yet, hey. Please, Ben, you promised your mum you'd stay.'

I DRIVE BEN HOME, taking a shortcut past the woods. I say little, trying to mind my own business. As we pass Argoed Farm, Ben covers his face with his hand. 'Shit,' he says, and slumps into his seat.

'What's up?' I ask.

Then I see him, Myatt, pointing at us from across the road. He shouts something, but I put my foot down and just about beat the lights.

I drive in silence for a while and then say. 'What the hell was all that about?'

'Stuff,' Ben says.

'Stuff?'

'Yeah, some shit I forgot to do.'

'Just keep out of his way for a while then. Stay in tonight. I'll pick you up at your house in the morning.'

Ben just looks at me, shaking his head, as though that's the worst thing anyone could do.

IT'S the sudden noise that wakes me, then the hushed voices, making my heart skip a beat. I put on my jeans. Grab my gun from beneath the mattress. It's a Glock replica, shoots nothing but pellets. But only a trained eye could tell the difference.

'Get out of my house,' I shout, hoping it's enough to scare them.

I stomp onto the landing, gaze down the stairs and see three masked faces staring up at me. I point the gun at them, trying to stop my hand from shaking. For a second, the one with the baseball bat considers his options. Thankfully, he scurries after his mates through the door. I creep downstairs, still holding the gun in case one of them has stayed behind.

They've left the living room light on and sprayed DEAD MAN across the walls. They've ripped up all my photographs, smashed Mum's porcelain figurines, and someone's shat on the floor.

I slump onto the sofa, thirsting for a beer. That foul smell they've left behind infects the air like poison. I see a face at the window, and to my relief it's Jordy.

I let him in.

'Jesus,' he says, staring at the graffiti on the wall.

He glances at the shit on the carpet. 'I was out walking, saw your light on.'

I take a deep breath, ask if he wants a cup of tea.

He follows me into the kitchen, his face pale beneath the halogen light.

He looks through the window. 'Who's done this then?'

'Who do you think?'

'Myatt?'

'Yeah, I've had a few run-ins with him lately.'

'What about?'

'Tina's boy, Ben.'

'Oh,' he says.

We watch the kettle boil, waiting for it to click.

We take our tea into the living room. The place looks a mess, and I know it's never going to feel the same.

Jordy shuffles in his chair and doesn't know where to look. 'You gonna call the police, Jase?'

'Shit no, like they'll be any help.'

'That Myatt's a lunatic. I saw him hit a guy with a hammer once, fractured his skull. He's fond of teenage girls, you know, boys too. I see him down the valley most nights, around midnight, walking his stupid dog.'

I nod. 'Yeah, I've seen him too.'

TINA IS STANDING by the gate when I arrive at Ben's the next morning. She hurries over to me, and I quickly wind down the window.

'You look awful, Tina.'

'So would you, if you'd spent half the night in A&E.'

'Why? What have you done?'

'Not me, it's Ben. He went out last night. He's in a right bloody mess. Someone's given him a hiding.'

'Myatt?'

'Probably, but Ben's refusing to say.'

'Can I see him?'

'Not now, Jase, maybe later.'

WHEN I GET TO WORK, I don't tell Berry much. I just say Ben's not feeling well.

'What did you say was wrong with him?' Berry keeps asking.

'I didn't. All Tina said was that the boy's in a bad way.'

'He looked fine to me last night. He must have caught a bug this morning.'

'Must have,' I say, and turn up the radio.

I hardly say a word all day. I just try to work through it. Berry knows there's something wrong but has the sense to keep his distance. He waits until we're closing up before he asks me. 'You all right, Jase? You've been acting strange all day.'

'I'm okay. I haven't slept much that's all. Someone broke into my house.'

Berry sets the alarm. 'Hell, why didn't you tell me?'

'It was only kids; it's nothing that can't be fixed.'

He rests a hand on my shoulder. 'Come and eat at mine then. Save you being on your own.'

'Thanks, but I've got things to do.'

Berry loses his smile. 'Good things I hope?'

I SPEND THE EVENING ALONE, drinking whisky, dark thoughts stirring inside me. The alcohol is gradually giving me the courage for what I need to do.

Whenever the doubt creeps in I picture the state of Stevey's face, which reminds me of Ben.

I peer from behind the curtain, hiding in the shadows.

Myatt's house is all lit up and, as always, the music's blaring. I watch the place for hours, seeing the druggies come and go. Sometimes Myatt comes outside, laughing too loud, wagging his bony finger. But whenever he glances up at my window, I make sure he doesn't see me.

He takes his dog for a walk just before midnight. He goes alone, so I put on my coat and follow.

Myatt takes a shortcut through the level. I keep well behind, allowing him some distance. He takes the valley path, and I follow him as far as the Flour Mill Pool. Then I sit on the wall, waiting for him to come full circle.

The moon shines bright, reminding me of that snowy December night, sixteen years ago. Stevey and I left the party early. We took a shortcut through the woods, to see whether the mill pools were frozen. A bloated moon lit up the sky, gleaming across the whiteness of the trees. Our every breath was frosted. Neither of us seemed bothered by the cold. We drank so much that night, and Stevey wouldn't stop talking. Finally, I told him to shut up, said he was getting on my nerves.

'I'll do what I want,' he said. 'Who are you to tell me what to do?'

'Well say something interesting then, something worth listening to.'

'Plenty of people like to hear what I've got to say. You'd be surprised.'

'Sure, like who?'

Stevey looked me in the eye, 'Tina, for one.'

'Tina? What have you been drinking? Why the hell would Tina want to listen to you?'

'Because I've been seeing her.'

'Bullshit.'

'I have, Tuesdays and Thursdays. Last Sunday I even stayed over at her house.'

I forced a laugh, but my heart was thumping. 'I'll give you one thing, Stevey, you've got a great imagination.'

Stevey lit a cigarette, blew the smoke straight at me. 'I know you've liked Tina for years, so saying yes to her wasn't easy.'

'Bullshit, whatever you're taking is messing around with your head.'

'I'm not lying. Tina's been coming on to me for weeks. The girl can't get enough of me.'

I took my hands out of my pockets. 'Tina's too nice for you. She wouldn't piss on you if you were on fire.'

Stevey undid the top buttons of his shirt and showed me the gold chain around his neck. 'Why did she give me this then?'

'Yeah, right.'

'She did.'

'When?'

'After I slept with her the other night.'

'You need to watch your mouth. You shouldn't talk about her like that.'

Stevey smiled. 'Or you'll do what? She loves it when I talk dirty.'

I punched him then. Jealousy, rage, disbelief, call it what you like. He fell backwards, cracking his head against the ice. He lay in a coma for weeks. The local papers said I saved him. Local Hero they wrote, and to this day, everyone still thinks he slipped. Sometimes I wonder if the old Stevey is lost somewhere in a dream. Desperate to wake up, so he can take care of Tina and their son.

When I hear Myatt trudging up the path, I creep out from the shadows. I strike him from the back, split his skull wide open. He's dead before he hits the ground. Like my dad used to say, only fools and frightened men give you a warning.

His dog looks up at me, and then runs off, and scampers through the woods.

I drag Myatt's body down to the pool, push his face into the water. By tomorrow morning, news of his death will be all over town. It was dealers from Liverpool they'll say, sending out a warning. But who's to say otherwise?

I mean, history's never written by the dead.

ALL THE HUNGRY GHOSTS

Four days passed and still no news of Johnny. Cai once read it could take several months. There were so many variables, the current, the tide, how heavily the body was weighted. It also depended on how far the body drifted out and how long the sea claimed it. As a boy, he heard so many tales of the sea's devilry. He lay awake for hours, listening to the distant waves, imagining the murmur of ghosts.

The rain, having plagued the town all morning, finally stopped by the time he got to Morgan's house. The grey streets still bruised by its memory. Morgan's young Asian bride greeted Cai at the door, offering him her hand; her fingers childlike as they brushed across his palm. She tried to speak but struggled to get her words out. Cai just nodded, feeling the tenderness of her smile as he followed her into the house. She led him down the hallway, hair shining beneath the morning light.

Morgan didn't stand when Cai entered the room. The old man remained slumped on the sofa; the bulk of him swaddled in a towelling robe. 'You're late,' he said and threw down his paper.

Cai kept quiet and sat in the chair opposite, shaking his head when Morgan offered him a cigarette. Morgan's new bride sat at the end of the sofa, shuffling closer as he patted the cushion next to him.

'Congratulations,' Cai said.

Morgan smiled then nodded, slowly, like an old king desperate to appear humble.

'Was it a big wedding?' Cai asked.

Morgan sighed. 'Big enough, just me, Lanfen and her family.'

'I guess she misses them.'

'I suppose, but they've all done pretty well out of it.'

As Morgan fell silent, Cai glanced around the room. It felt cleaner somehow, brighter too. His eyes fixed on the coffee table and then on an assortment of paper shapes piled on top of it. They'd been cut out from a magazine. There was a necklace, a wristwatch, and the rough outline of a car still caught in the scissors' bite.

'How was China?' he said.

Morgan caressed his throat. 'Dusty.' He coughed and leaned closer, his eyes narrowing. 'Speaking of China, I heard you sorted out our little problem, up at the Red Dragon.'

Cai nodded, lowering his eyes as he pictured Johnny's face.

Morgan narrowed his eyes. 'What's wrong?'

'Nothing.'

Morgan sat up. 'Lanfen,' he shouted and pointed to the door.

Lanfen stood, gathered up her paper shapes and skittered out to the hall.

'She's well trained,' Cai joked.

Morgan grimaced then slumped back into the sofa. 'She knows hardly any English. That's why I have to point things out to her.'

Cai looked away, the slyness of Morgan's smile getting the better of him.

'What's everyone saying about this?' Morgan asked.

'About what?'

Morgan raised his eyes. 'Lanfen, of course. My matrimonial bliss.'

Cai considered the question. 'Everyone was surprised, I guess. We knew you'd met someone online, but when you announced you were getting married, well, it all came as a bit of a shock.'

'And what else was said?'

Cai stared at his hands. 'You know, the usual stuff.'

'What stuff?'

'Internet bride, all that kind of crap.'

Morgan gazed at the photographs on the mantelpiece. 'I've been a widower for too long. Isn't a man like me entitled to some happiness?'

Cai remained silent, wondering what a man such as Morgan was entitled. The old man earned the name Mad Morgan. He made his money in the '80s from loan sharking and rented accommodation. These days he was a respectable businessman, bluffing his way through council contracts. Things didn't always go to plan. That's when Cai got involved, running the old man's errands up and down the North Wales coast.

'You've got the look,' Morgan told him, all those years ago. That burn on the side of your face, it makes people uncomfortable. Let's make some money, the old man said.

Show these luckless bastards that Mad Morgan's still capable.

It excited Cai at the time. He was young; he didn't know what else to do. Over the years, Morgan's hold on him grew tighter, using it as a leash whenever Cai threatened to leave. Now Morgan had a wife, a friendless soul who didn't even have the words to protest.

MORGAN PUSHED himself up from the sofa. 'Do you want a drink?' sighing when Cai shook his head. He trudged over to the sideboard, his hand shaking while he poured himself a whisky. 'You didn't have any trouble at the Red Dragon?'

Cai shook his head. 'Why? Is there a problem?'

'Not really. Big Bryn called me an hour ago, confirming he'd dropped his tender.'

'What else did he say?'

'Oh, this and that. He spoke mostly about his nephew, Johnny.'

Cai's heart pounded in his throat. 'What about him?'

Morgan cast him a glance. 'He's gone missing, apparently. Bryn asked if I knew anything about it.'

Morgan slumped down on the sofa. He sat quietly, swirling the whisky around his glass. 'I want you to do me a favour.'

Cai nodded.

'I want you to drive us around for a while, tomorrow morning, nowhere far, just enough for Lanfen to get a sense of the place.'

'I'm a chauffeur now?'

Morgan cleared his throat. 'I guess if that's what you want to call it. It's a good idea, don't you think?'

'And why would I think that?'

'It'll keep you out of mischief, and that's better for both of us.'

BENEATH A STARLESS NIGHT SKY, Cai drove home. The river drew him closer, leading him to the water's edge. He took a left past the railway bridge, slowing down as the road narrowed. To a passing stranger, the road appeared to lead nowhere, nothing more than an industrial cul-de-sac, a stretch of pot-holed tarmac with a fence on either side. Beyond the brambles and the incessant hum of the generator was the River Dee, its blue-brown tidal mouth bleeding into the Irish Sea.

He reversed into a parking bay. The headlights' beam revealed two young lovers sitting in the car opposite. It had been four nights now since he last saw Johnny. He recalled the scene. Johnny stood next to Cai at the bar, a young man, barely out of his teens, his smile brazen, and his eyes full of spite. Cai tried his best to ignore him. He sat quietly at a corner table, bathing his face in shadow.

Fifteen minutes later, and Big Bryn strode towards him. Bryn sat down, the wooden chair barely holding his weight. Cai handed him Morgan's note. Bryn read it slowly, as if every word were a strain. 'This is a little less than we agreed.'

Cai shrugged. 'I know nothing about that. You'll have to speak with Morgan.'

'Do you have it with you?'

Cai nodded, watching him carefully.

Bryn stood. 'Let's continue up in the flat,' he said, then raised his arm and beckoned Cai to follow.

As they made their way upstairs, Johnny followed them. Cai could smell his aftershave, its heady cheapness hounding him like a terrible memory. The room was warm, cosy almost. Cai sat back into a chair, staring up at the painting that hung above the fireplace. The colour of the sky caught his attention, long streaks of vermilion broken by scatters of pink. The sun was a tired red eye, bleeding across the canvas.

'Let's have it then,' Bryn said, smiling as Cai threw him the package.

Johnny entered the room and stood behind Bryn's chair. Bryn ripped open the package, his eyelids flickering as he counted through the wad of notes. 'I'm only pulling out because Morgan made me a good offer. If that old fool wants to play gangsters that's up to him.'

Cai smiled. 'What do you mean?'

'Sending you here as if you're a threat.'

Johnny laughed, his eyes widening with excitement. 'It's the burnt skin on his face. It scares people. They think he's a freak.'

Bryn sighed. 'I'm sorry about my nephew, but Johnny has his mother's mouth, I'm afraid.'

Cai nodded. 'No problem, I'm sure someone close it soon enough.'

As Johnny leapt from behind the chair, Bryn blocked his way, his fingers outstretched, pressing into Johnny's chest.

'Behave yourself,' Bryn shouted, the menace in his voice silencing his nephew.

Cai stood up, ignoring Johnny's glare.

'Tell Morgan,' Bryn said, 'that I'm pulling out. If he wants to waste his money on a no profit tender, then that's his business. But the pair of you would do well to stop acting as if you owned the place. You're not the only ones in this town who can play Cowboys and Indians.'

Cai nodded, placing his hands in his pockets before going downstairs.

He strode to his car, noticing Bryn's jeep was parked in the bay opposite. Then he drove into the darkness, making his way to the river.

There were no other cars parked at the estuary that night, and Cai was happy to be alone there. He went for a walk, strolling along the seawall path. The tide was in, swelling over the sandbanks. He watched it for a while, sweeping across the distant marshes. He couldn't remember what made him turn around, a sense of something perhaps, an evil omen. For a moment, he thought it was a ghost, a will-o'-the-wisp weaving through the jagged rocks. Then he realised it was Johnny, tall and gaunt, his face shining from the glow of his cigarette.

Cai drew his hands from his pockets as Johnny walked towards him.

When he tried to pass, Johnny blocked his way. The boy placed his hands on Cai's shoulders, pushing his face closer. Johnny's breath smelt bad, a mix of whisky and cigarettes. 'You're an easy one to find,' he said.

Cai stared into Johnny's eyes. The boy looked different close up. He often found that with people's faces, the slightest detail reshaping their appearance. With Johnny, it was the paleness of his skin, the hollow cheeks, making him ghostlike.

'What do you want?' Cai said.

'I wanna give you an opportunity.'

'For what?'

Johnny grinned. 'To shut me up, give me that slap you said I needed.'

Johnny stretched out his arms, blocking Cai as he tried to pass.

'Just leave it alone,' Cai said.

But Johnny was having none of it. 'I knew you were full

of shit. I've seen the way you walk around, you and that old fool, Morgan.'

'Leave it,' Cai shouted, and Johnny was silent.

It was a moment of caution, and Johnny quickly regained his confidence.

'Come on, shut me up,' Johnny kept shouting, his finger prodding Cai's chest.

Cai grabbed hold of Johnny's hand, twisting it back until the boy screamed. Johnny threw a punch, a misguided swoop, grazing the side of Cai's ear. With the back of his hand, Cai slapped Johnny to the ground. The boy looked emaciated, outstretched, his body like a sack of bones.

Dazed only for a moment, Johnny scrambled to his feet, blood trickling from his nose and mouth.

'I'm gonna kill you,' Johnny shouted, and pulled out a gun, blue-grey steel glinting as it caught the light.

Cai lunged towards him. He grabbed Johnny by the lapels and hurled him like a rag. The boy tumbled across the sand, his head cracking against the rocks. Johnny lay still, his spindly arms raised above his head. Cai stood over him, staring at the boy's face. Even in death Johnny looked defiant, his eyes raised indignantly and his thin lips half-smiling.

When Cai pulled into Morgan's drive, the old man was outside smoking a cigarette. Morgan barely acknowledged him, looking away as Cai stepped out of the car. The old man seemed different. There was a glint in his eyes, something secret behind his smile.

There was no sign of Lanfen as Cai followed Morgan inside, just her scent lingering in the hallway.

'Wait for me in there,' Morgan said and pointed towards

the lounge. The room smelt stale, the fireplace strewn with cigarette stumps and a dried spill of whisky bled from a broken glass. Morgan's robe lay spread across the carpet. Lying next to it was Lanfen's slip, a fold of bronze silk, torn along the seam and shed like an unwanted skin.

Lanfen entered the room like a shadow, her small dark shape skulking across the carpet. She didn't return Cai's smile. Instead, she fixed her gaze on the table and its assortment of paper shapes. She edged towards them, wincing as she knelt. She tidied them up, her hands shaking as she carefully folded each shape. Cai could have watched her all morning and had half a mind to join her. Lanfen stood and then walked over to the window, slowly drawing back the curtains and bathing the room in light. Cai smiled as she turned to face him, the sadness in her eyes holding him silent. He wanted to reach out to her. He felt cleaner when she was this close, and the darkness of recent days faded. Then he noticed the bruises on her arms and the spots of blood on her clothes. Lanfen shut her eyes, lowering her head in shame.

When Cai heard Morgan hurrying down the stairs, he stepped into the hallway. Cai folded his arms, blocking the old man's path.

'What the hell's wrong with you?' Morgan said.

Cai shrugged. 'I don't know. You tell me?'

'Tell you about what, exactly?'

'Whether Lanfen's okay, she seems a little—'

'She's all right,' Morgan said, reaching into his pocket and pulling out his pack of cigarettes. Cai watched as Morgan fired up his lighter, the yellow flame reflected in the old man's eyes. 'Not that it's any of your business.'

They stared at each other in silence as Lanfen inched into the hallway. She crept upstairs, squirming as Morgan brushed past her. The old man shook his head, grimacing at her bundle of shapes.

'What does she do with those?' Cai asked.

'Hungry ghosts,' Morgan said, making his way into the lounge.

Cai followed, the words unsettling him. 'Ghosts?'

Morgan shook his head. 'Some crap about the fifteenth day of the lunar month.' He raised his eyes. 'Some expat told me about it in a bar. It's a common thing over there apparently, especially in the poorer parts of the South.'

'What's it all about?'

Morgan smiled. 'They believe it's when we're visited by the dead, and we're supposed to feed them, to stop them cursing us.'

'How?'

Morgan flicked his ash on the carpet. 'With gifts, TVs, watches, they make them out of paper, and then burn them in the streets.'

Cai stared at him.

'Stupid, hey, Lanfen's been pestering me about it ever since we got back.'

'How?'

'By pointing at those shapes of hers and then taking hold of my lighter.'

'Why don't you just let her burn them? I don't suppose it could do any harm.'

'No way, I'm not having my wife acting like a lunatic.'

THE TOUR STARTED with a drive through town, past the pound shops, the pubs, and the shabby cafeterias. Morgan was in his element, waving from the window, acting as if he owned the place. Now and then, Lanfen threw Cai a glance, her dark eyes full of sorrow. Morgan was bouncing, raising his voice, and telling the same old stories. Eventually, the old man lost interest, complaining he was thirsty and demanding Cai pull into the nearest pub.

'It's best that you wait in the car,' Morgan said. 'We won't be long. I just want to show off my new wife.'

While Cai waited, all he could think about was Johnny and what he was going to do with his gun. Even Lanfen's smile couldn't rid Cai of his memories, and every time he closed his eyes, he pictured Johnny's face.

Hours later, his arm wrapped around Lanfen's shoulder, Morgan staggered back to the car. Cai took a deep breath. He hated it when Morgan drank, the unrelenting boasts and the endless insults.

'Would Lanfen like to sit up front?' Cai said. 'I'll drive through the hills if you like, show her some of the sights.'

Morgan belched, filling the air with the smell of whisky. 'She's all right where she is. You just concentrate on your driving.'

Cai eased the car onto the road, pressing harder on the gas. He watched Morgan from the rearview mirror. The old man pulled Lanfen closer, his liver-spotted hand reaching into her blouse. Cai slammed down on the brakes, the car's sudden jolt hurling Morgan forward onto the floor.

'For Christ's sake,' Morgan shouted. 'What the hell are you up to?'

'Sorry. It was a rabbit. The stupid little thing ran out in front of me.'

Cai switched on the hazard lights and jumped out of the car. He opened the backdoor, motioning Lanfen towards him. She moved quickly, Morgan groaning as she climbed over him. Cai took hold of her arm and guided her to the front.

The old man was lighter than he expected, and with one swift tug, Cai lifted him back into the seat. Morgan looked exhausted, the life drained from him. He took out his handkerchief, dabbing it across his brow.

'Stretch out for a bit,' Cai said. 'Have a rest until we get back.'

Morgan glared at him. 'You're a nurse now, are you?' The old man scrunched his face. 'I think I've done something to my ankle. It was fine until she jumped all over it.'

'Try to rest,' Cai said, slamming the door behind him.

Despite the old man's impatience, Cai drove slowly. He took the long route back, Lanfen sitting next to him. Each time Cai glanced at her, he caught her staring. There was a knowing look in her eyes, and for once she was smiling.

Now at the crossroads, Cai took a left, heading down a narrow lane that led to the fisheries. Morgan took a swig from his hip flask. 'Where are you going? We should have been back ages ago.'

'There's a field at the end of this road,' Cai said. 'I thought it would be a good spot for Lanfen to burn her shapes.'

The old man shook his head and pointed at the window. 'You're getting as crazy as she is, just turn around in that driveway.'

Cai did as instructed. There was little point in arguing. The drunker the old man got, the more determined he became to shout you down.

'It's not that much quicker,' Cai said, in a last act of defiance.

Morgan sighed. 'Just get me home. You're the last person I'd ask for an opinion.'

Now on the old Coast Road, Cai drove faster. The night was quiet, the moon peering through the trees. Morgan looked pleased with himself, stretched out like a lord, contentedly drinking. 'What's wrong with you tonight, Cai? I thought you'd want to keep a low profile.'

Cai kept his eyes on the road. 'What's that supposed to mean?'

'You know what it means. A certain friend of ours is linking you to Johnny.'

Cai pressed harder on the gas, silent as the car raced through the ebbing light.

IT TOOK Cai ages to get Morgan out of the car. The old man kept struggling, insisting he could help himself. When Cai finally got Morgan into the house, he lifted him onto the sofa. Lanfen took Morgan's jacket, then pulled off his shoes and socks. Morgan's feet reeked of sweat, and his toenails were yellow stubs.

Morgan caught sight of Cai's disgust. 'Have you looked in the mirror, lately?'

Cai stepped away from him, ambling over to the sideboard. He poured out a glass of whisky and handed it to Morgan.

'You're not a bad lad,' Morgan said. 'Don't worry about Big Bryn. I'll sort it.'

Cai forced a smile. 'Best have a few more of those. They'll help with that ankle.'

Encouraging Morgan to drink was the best thing Cai could do for Lanfen. Get the old man smashed until his body collapsed into sleep.

Lanfen knelt at the table, flicking through a magazine. She tore out one page, an advert for a lady's watch. She picked up the scissors, eyeing Morgan as she cut.

The old man watched her for a moment, sighing into his empty glass.

'Fancy another?' Cai asked.

Morgan shook his head. 'No, I've had enough.' He traced the rim of the glass with his finger. 'I'm a married man now. I need to keep my strength up.'

Lanfen blushed as the old man stared at her, the worry in her eyes thickening the beat of Cai's heart.

'If that's the case,' Cai said. 'Why don't you rest a while? I can drive Lanfen somewhere, let her burn those shapes.'

'Why do you keep going on about those things? Why's it so important to you?'

Cai held up his hands. 'Hey, I'm only trying to help. You said yourself she's been pestering you.'

Morgan frowned, then wiped his hand across his forehead. 'Go on then, but make sure no one sees you.'

Cai struggled not to smile, but somehow, he managed it. He tapped Lanfen's shoulder and pointed at the paper shapes. She looked confused at first until Cai held out his palm and struck it with an imaginary match. It was the happiest he'd seen her. She threw back her head, filling the room with laughter. Then she hugged him, kissing the side of his face. Cai felt warm inside, pleased with himself until he caught sight of the old man staring.

'We won't be long,' Cai said, trying his best to ignore him.

But Morgan stopped smiling. 'You know what, I've changed my mind. Let's do it another time. I could do with an early night.'

'But I've just told her. We can't–'

Morgan slammed his glass on the table. 'Don't tell me what I can and cannot do.'

'But–'

'I can do what I like.'

As Cai shuffled to the door, Lanfen followed. Morgan kept calling her name, but she refused to turn around. Cai shook his head and pointed her towards the sofa. Lanfen held out her hands, offering him her paper shapes.

'I'm sorry,' Cai whispered, and looked at Morgan.

The old man sat up, folding his flabby arms. When Lanfen saw the ugliness of Morgan's smile, she lunged towards him. Morgan grabbed her wrists and threw her on the table. She fell back on the glass surface, spreading her hands to support herself. For a moment, Cai just stood there, dumbstruck, watching the paper shapes fluttering down to the carpet.

'Pick that little whore up,' Morgan said, wiping the sweat from his brow.

Tears streamed down Lanfen's face, her voice hoarse as she bellowed out her curses. She leapt onto Morgan's chest, battering his face with her fists. This time, Morgan grabbed her throat, grinning as he choked the life from her. Cai leaned on the sofa, taking hold of Morgan's hands and wrenching them from Lanfen's windpipe.

'Get the hell off me,' the old man shouted.

Cai grabbed Morgan's wrists. 'Calm down then.'

'You calm down,' Morgan said and spat into Cai's face. Cai stared into the old man's eyes, warm saliva trickling down his cheek.

'You better watch yourself,' Morgan said, wheezing. 'None of us are stupid, you know. It doesn't take a genius to work out what happened to Johnny. One word from me and–'

Cai grabbed Morgan's throat, tightening his grip, squeezing harder, watching the fire wither from the old man's eyes. You stole my youth from me, he thought, blackened any good I ever had.

CAI IMAGINED Morgan would be an uncompromising ghost, more vindictive in spirit than he ever was in the flesh. Cai glanced across at Lanfen, her eyes meeting his own. She led Cai slowly to a chair, her soft hands guiding him through the darkness. How quickly the night came, an unwanted guest, feasting on the day's sorrow. Lanfen looked older in the half-light, as if aged by the spirits that cursed her. She lifted Cai's hand to her mouth, gracing it with a kiss. Cai drew her close, holding her tighter, as someone, something, hammered against the front door. Cai placed a finger on his lips, breathless, as the knocking grew fiercer.

'Morgan,' the voice kept shouting, 'open this door, man.'

For a moment, Cai thought it was Johnny's ghost, spewed out by the river and sent to haunt him. Then Cai smiled to himself, realising it was the boy's uncle.

'Morgan,' Bryn kept shouting. 'Wake up, man. I need to talk to you.'

Cai closed his eyes, Lanfen's heart beating against his chest.

They held each other through it all, silent among every threat.

After twenty minutes, Bryn finally gave up. Cai waited for a while, listening for the sound of Bryn's jeep before switching on the light. He drew back the curtains, his heart almost missing a beat as Morgan's reflection stared at him in the window.

· · ·

CAI CARRIED Morgan's body to the car, laying it belly-up on the backseat. Then he covered it with a blanket, Morgan's head tilting to one side. Cai stood outside for a moment, taking in the midnight air. He gazed at the distant houses and their collection of orange lights. Then the idea came to him, hitting him like a slap from nowhere. Cai rushed over to the back of the car and flipped open the boot. He ploughed through Morgan's junk, stopping when he found the fuel can. He threw it in the backseat, gently closing the boot so as not to draw attention to himself.

When Cai got back inside, Lanfen was waiting for him in the hall. She looked so pale, smiling like the friendliest of ghosts. Cai clenched his fists, rocking them from side to side as if steering an invisible wheel. Lanfen nodded and handed him her paper shapes. Cai smiled at her, then reached into his pocket and pulled out Morgan's lighter. 'Everything's going to be fine.'

He knew his words held no meaning, but something in his voice seemed to reassure her. Cai lowered his head, his eyes closing as they kissed.

CAI DROVE a steady sixty along the deserted A-road, Lanfen's perfume covering him like a second skin. This was how it felt to be wanted. These were the feelings of the loved. Cai pulled into the all-night garage, got out of the car, and started filling the can with petrol. As he waited, he noticed a silver Land Rover parked in the lay-by opposite. He didn't recognise the number plate and couldn't make out who sat beyond the tinted glass.

After paying for the petrol, Cai hurried back to his car. He drove to the river, always checking behind him. Whenever Cai glanced into the mirror, he caught sight of Morgan's body. He pictured the old man burning, Morgan's last gift, a fire to appease all hungers.

It was almost dawn as Cai took a left onto the Old Dock Road, a whiskery light ageing the darkness. He wound down the window, inhaling the morning's promise. With the estuary in his sights, Cai drove faster, speeding through the fading shadows. Then, just as Cai approached the seawall, the Land Rover appeared from nowhere, cutting him up and dazzling him with its headlights. Cai slammed on the brakes, flipping the car over and rolling it across the sand.

WHEN HE EVENTUALLY OPENED HIS eyes, Cai found himself upside down, struggling to breathe, cold steel pressing against his chest. Morgan's body had been hurled against the window; his face masked with blood and pellets of shattered glass.

Cai listened to the seabird mewling above, and the distant tide murmuring to the rasp of his breath. Petrol fumes flooded his senses, stinging his eyes, and burning through his nose and throat. Then he caught sight of the punctured can, its trickle of clear liquid seeping into the paper shapes.

For a moment, Cai thought the man staring down at him was Johnny's ghost. Older now, the boy's hollow cheeks were bloated and aged by the sea. Big Bryn shook his head, his fingers bloodless as he raked them through his hair. Cai didn't recognise the other man. A relative, he guessed, both men sharing that same swarthy look.

Big Bryn rested on his haunches. 'We're going to cut you out, then find out what happened to Johnny.'

As the two men shifted out of sight, Cai pictured Lanfen, the memory of their kiss reminding him of his promise.

Slowly, Cai raised his arm, his shoulder crunching, the pain surging down to his fingers. He released his seatbelt, his body slumping against the dashboard. Cai fumbled in his pocket, sighing with relief as his hand smoothed across Morgan's lighter. He held it to his face, sparking it up with his thumb. The flame purred, shimmying in front of his eyes. With one last excruciating stretch, he held the lighter to the can. The fire spread quickly, burning the paper shapes, feeding the hungry ghosts, and peppering the sky with ash.

THIS LAND OF THE STRANGE

Jernegan knew they'd come. She left enough clues for them to find her. Swain wanted her dead, so it was only a matter of time. The moment she stepped off the bus and sniffed the air, such thoughts left her, abandoning her to the smell of the soil, the pines, and the faint tang of the sea.

She took in the hills, the sky, and the faraway mountains, knowing this was the land that never changed, the place where she longed to be.

Thirty summers she waited, and with the passing of each season, convinced herself it was special, magical even, the gradual reshaping of her memories telling her a better story.

With her suitcase under her arm, Jernegan followed the B-road into town. The evening light ebbed and the sun, like a tired red eye, slunk behind the watchful trees.

WHEN JERNEGAN REACHED THE TOWN, the sun surrendered to the darkness, its last pale lick of light settling over the hills.

She was a girl when she last walked these streets. The narrow pavements looked unaltered, their kerbstones jutting out like rows of crooked teeth. It was as though the town were laughing at her, mocking her return.

She walked beneath the streetlights, her shadow, like the girl she once was, striding ahead of her.

All those years ago the town provided everything, supplying groceries, hardware, electronics, men's and women's clothing. Now, only a few shops remained, newsagents, card shops, and empty cafes. The grey stone wall outside the bank had disappeared. Jernegan loitered there as a girl, perching on the railings, smoking her stolen cigarettes.

Even Woolworths was gone. The building gutted, refurbished, converted into a Gastro pub. As a teenager, every Saturday morning Jernegan would buy a record from there, listening to it on her mother's Hi-Fi, playing it over and over, until she memorised every word.

'*The heart finds a special place for the old songs,*' Connie once told her.

Jernegan breathed deeply, the knot in her stomach tightening.

JERNEGAN CONTINUED ALONG THE PAVEMENT, following it through town, then up Station Hill to the houses along its banks. The house where she was born was now a guesthouse. its facias and cladding painted yellow, and its pebble-dashed walls the colour of curdled cream. The rusty gate creaked open. Jernegan marched down the path and rang the doorbell. Light spilled onto the step, illuminating the face of the man standing in the doorway. The old man reminded her of Swain, with his slicked back hair, trimmed white beard, potbelly, and rounded shoulders. It lasted only a second, the kindness of the old man's smile quickly breaking the illusion.

'I'd like a room, please,' Jernegan said.

The old man nodded. 'You've come to the right place, Miss. Come in,' he said, and Jernegan followed him into the hall.

The place had a classic feel to it, a B&B of old, like something from the 1930s. The reception area was a makeshift wooden booth next to the kitchen door. The old man stepped inside the booth and sat on a swivel chair. He switched on the lamp, half of his face masked by shadow.

'What's the name?' he said, grabbing hold of his pen.

'Jernegan.'

'One R or two?'

'One.'

The old man beamed. 'You're in luck. You've a choice of four rooms; we've almost an empty house.'

Jernegan stepped aside, allowing the man to pass.

The old man led her upstairs, pausing when they reached the landing. 'The rooms at the back are the quietest. They look out across the valley. It's one hell of a view, especially when it isn't raining.'

Jernegan nodded to the door on her left. 'How about this one?'

'Good choice, and seeing as we're so quiet, I'll only charge you the single rate.'

Jernegan nodded, said good night, then stepped into the room.

. . .

IT WAS HER PARENTS' room. Now, only the view of the valley was recognisable. Jernegan's brother sold the place years ago. God knows how many strangers slept here since.

She took off her jacket and placed it on the chair, then rolled up her sleeves, grabbed her suitcase and dumped it on the bed. She flipped back the lid and stared at it. She bought the walking gear years ago, for a holiday destined never to be, a tour of her beloved Wales, something she and Connie often talked about. She had a rucksack, a waterproof jacket, trousers, and boots, even had a thermal hat and scarf.

She hung up her clothes, then took out her knife and cut through the suitcase lining.

She packed the money tight, twenty rubber-banded stacks of £5000, sealed in its own plastic bag.

She put the money in her rucksack, then undressed, pausing before switching off the light.

With her gun by her side, she lay on the bed, her eyes closed, listening in the darkness.

Nighttime in the valley, the wind relentless and cold, the tide murmuring beyond the trees, just like the whisper of Connie's voice, tender, but forever calling.

She recalled how Connie teased her. 'Welshwoman of the hills,' Connie used to say, 'always pining for her land of the strange.'

Lately, thinking of Connie always reminded Jernegan of Swain. Jernegan first met Swain in London, in '82, introduced by an associate, a lowlife named Grubb. Grubb vouched Jernegan was an excellent driver, said she was handy, too. Swain remained silent, ignoring Grubb, his shark eyes fixed on Jernegan.

'Journeyman?' he said.

'Jern-e-gan.'

'What are you, Irish?'

'Welsh.'

'You got a clean licence?'

Jernegan nodded.

Swain eyed her dismissively. 'We don't have a lot of women on the payroll. Come to the White Swan tonight. Ask for Cole and Franklin. I've the perfect job for you.'

Swain's jealousy often got the better of him. A woman driver gave him peace of mind. He hired Jernegan that very night, told her to keep an eye on his wife, run her errands, drive her around town.

The gods blessed Connie Swain with conventional beauty, a tall blonde, both sassy and discreet, her elegance never faltering. She was sharp too, unashamedly smarter than all of them.

'Do you like to read, Jernegan?' was the first thing Connie asked her.

'I flick through the papers on a Sunday,' she said, 'catch up on the news and stuff.'

'What about books, novels and the like?'

'I've never really seen the point, Mrs. Swain.'

'Why's that?'

'I've enough problems of my own, without thinking about someone else's.'

Connie laughed, the words tickling her for days, and from that moment on she sat up front.

THE NEXT MORNING, as Jernegan walked down the stairs, the old man greeted her in the hallway. 'You're a heavy sleeper.'

Jernegan frowned. 'What makes you say that?'

'You slept through all the commotion.'

'What commotion?'

The old man chuckled. 'Exactly, your friends from down

south, ringing to see whether you'd arrived then turning up one o'clock this morning.'

'How many?'

'Two.'

'Mr. Swain?'

'Nope, a Mr. Cole and a Mr. Franklin. They're having breakfast, waiting for you to join them.'

The moment Jernegan stepped into the dining room, Franklin burst into laughter. 'Jesus, Jernegan, what the hell do you look like. Why are you dressed like that? You look like a rambler.'

Jernegan ignored him and sat at the table by the window. She watched the birds darting through the trees, then gazed at the black outline of the power station, and the sunlight bristling across the shore. When she looked away from the window, she caught Franklin staring at her, chewing with his mouth open.

Mad Franklin looked like a giant sitting in his chair, his shovel-like hands clutching his tiny knife and fork. Cole, too, appeared equally misplaced. Both men wore tailored black suits, yet they made an odd pairing. Franklin was tall and pale while Cole was short, his face choppy and flushed.

Franklin swallowed his food and belched into his fist. 'I wasn't expecting this town to be such a shithole, especially the way you used to go on about it. People here don't even sound Welsh; we could be anywhere in England.'

Jernegan glanced towards the window. 'We're on the border. England's just across the river.'

'There's some magnificent scenery, though,' added Cole, trying to mediate as always.

Franklin leaned back into his chair. 'It's all right, I suppose. But where are all the sheep, the forests, the mountains?'

'Close,' Jernegan said.

'How close?'

Jernegan shrugged. 'Ten to fifteen miles west.'

Franklin reached into his pocket and pulled out a cigarette.

'You can't smoke in here,' Jernegan said.

Franklin took a drag, the smoke curling around his fingers.

Jernegan scraped back her chair, eying both men as she stood. 'You ignorant prick. You've no respect for anyone.'

Franklin grinned. 'Did you see me lighting it? Relax, darling. It's an e-cig, nothing but vapour.'

'Very smart,' Jernegan said. 'I bet that impresses those young boyfriends of yours.'

Franklin sprang out of his chair, almost toppling the thing over. 'Cleverer than you, though, hey? At least I don't go taking things that don't belong to me.'

Jernegan stepped forward, stopping in her tracks as the old man shuffled through the doorway.

The old man started clearing the plates. 'It seems you're the only one who enjoys my food, Mr. Cole. These two have barely touched a scrap.'

Cole slapped his hands onto his gut. 'That's their loss. I enjoyed every bite.'

'Can I get you anything else?'

Cole shook his head. 'No thanks, I couldn't eat another thing. The three of us need to crack on. We've lots of unfinished business.'

WHILE FRANKLIN and Cole were upstairs, Jernegan took a bus timetable from reception and sneaked out through the back. She thumbed a lift into town, surprised by how easy it all was. She got dropped off at the bus stop and waited quietly by the road. Her plan was to get the A14 out of town, get off near the moors, and start hiking. Where she was headed to was undecided; she only hoped they would follow.

Jernegan kept watching the road. Ten minutes passed. The wrong bus arrived, then another, each wasted second making her more anxious. When the A14 finally turned up, Cole's green BMW trailed behind it. Jernegan hurried onto the bus, paid her fare, and sat in the back row. As the bus pulled away, Jernegan glimpsed Franklin's eyes. A cold, dark stare she'd tolerated far too long.

'That Franklin scares me,' Connie once confessed. 'Oh, he's polite enough, but there's something about him.'

Jernegan laughed it off at the time, telling her not to give it a second thought. She lied, of course. She was all too aware of Franklin's dark deeds. They infected her dreams like a poison.

THE BUS JERKED TO A STOP, waking Jernegan from her daydream. She stared through the window, taking in the vast stretch of moorland and the big grey sky above.

'This is the stop for the Moors,' the driver shouted, 'you asked me to tell you.'

Jernegan glanced through the back window, watching the green BMW behind them. She grabbed her rucksack and hurried down the aisle. 'Any more stops further down? This isn't where I want to go.'

The driver mumbled something, then pulled back onto the road. Jernegan remained standing, her attention flitting between the moors and the line of traffic behind them.

'Why doesn't that bloody BMW overtake?' the driver

said. 'I keep slowing down for him.'

The bus picked up speed. A white van, appearing from nowhere, took advantage of the gap. The bus and the van beat the lights, leaving the traffic behind them. As the gap widened, Jernegan saw her chance. 'Drop me off here,' she said, pointing to a remote bus stop.

The driver sighed, then pulled into a lay-by.

The minute the doors opened, Jernegan leapt off the bus. She raced across the road, clambered over the fence, and started following the sheep trail, meandering through the bracken, towards the wooded valley along the moorland fringes. The hill grew steeper, forcing her to climb. Jernegan felt every sharp intake of breath and the heather prickling across her skin. A stiff wind wailed through the sodden grass, then, like the rapid crash of thunder, she heard gunshots.

Jernegan jogged up the hill, never daring to look back, moving faster, breathing harder.

WHEN SHE REACHED THE VALLEY, Jernegan stopped to catch her breath, the crisp air rolling across her tongue. A red kite watched her from above, its wings outstretched, hovering on the breeze.

Franklin and Cole wouldn't be far behind, providing they weren't lost.

Jernegan marched towards the trees, then stepped into the woods, breathing deeply, inhaling the rich smell of pine. She kept walking, following the trail, her boots squelching in the mud. Occasionally, she gazed up at the sky, at the immense grey clouds sailing over her. She hoped the rain would draw them here, running for shelter, like two lambs to the slaughter.

The trail took her further into the woods, leading her to a small clearing. She scrambled down the bank, stopping when she reached the rock. The crag which stood just over fifty feet, provided plenty of edges and pockets, making it easy for Jernegan to climb.

When she reached the top, Jernegan looked across the trees. She could see for miles and, even when she turned to face the bushes behind her, she'd a clear view of the surrounding fields.

Jernegan sighed. 'Let them come,' she whispered.

JERNEGAN SAT ON THE GRASS, leaning against her rucksack. Behind her closed eyelids, she saw Connie's smile. Connie stood with her back to the car, soaking her face in light. It was to be their last time together, the weekend before Connie's *accident*. It had been an odd day from the start. The weather, which was so changeable, rain, hail, sunshine, put Connie in a pensive mood. 'I dread to think what my husband will do if he ever finds out about us.' She would say this from time to time, but that day she seemed more anxious.

'Swain hasn't got a clue,' Jernegan said. 'Stop worrying.'

'He's been more attentive lately, snooping around my room, asking lots of questions.'

Jernegan put her arm around her, and started talking about her beloved Wales, desperate to change the subject. She spoke of the tour they planned. How they'd do everything differently, even travel by bus.

This seemed to cheer Connie up. '*Public Transport*, isn't that a little down market?'

Jernigan smiled. 'I'm sick of driving you around; we'll get to take in the beautiful view.'

'If it's so beautiful, why did you leave?'

'Because nothing happens there, and that's why we're going back.'

Jernegan was cleaning Swain's car when she learned of Connie's death. Franklin broke the news, the big man appearing to gloat. 'The stupid bitch got run over this morning, died from a broken neck.'

At first, Jernegan just stared at him, her heart pounding inside her throat. 'That's so sad,' she said, clenching her fists, trying to stop her hands from shaking.

Franklin shrugged. 'I suppose, but she had it coming if you know what I mean. Mr. Swain asked me personally.'

'Why?'

Franklin grinned. 'You know how jealous that old man gets. He found a load of stuff written in her diary, a poem or something. Seems she was sleeping around.'

Jernegan didn't attend Connie's funeral. She was frightened of what she might do, kill someone, or sob her heart out. Instead, she drove to Swain's apartment, left the car in the driveway, and let herself in with her key. After clearing Swain's safe, Jernegan wandered into Connie's room. It felt as though Connie was still there, the sweet linger of her scent and the slight indent on her pillow. Jernegan browsed through Connie's hidden books, taking out the one she bought her. She laid it open on the bed, taking a deep breath before reading its inscription.

'*All my love, Jernegan,*' she whispered, '*p.s. come with me to the land of the strange.*'

JERNEGAN SIGHED, wiped the tears from her eyes, then gazed across the fields. Two black shapes trudged down the hill. One was tall and slim, the other short and broad. They reminded her of a cartoon, and it might have been comical if she hadn't known their intentions.

She rested on her haunches, watching her pursuers vanish into the woods. The wind carried Franklin's voice, faint at first, but growing louder.

Jernegan crept into the bushes and took the gun from her rucksack. The light was fading, but she guessed it would be at least two hours before dark. All she needed were two clear shots, and she'd be back in town by nightfall. She could hear them breathing now, loud and fast, as though both men were gasping for air. Then she glimpsed them on the bank.

Cole showed himself first, his hair dishevelled, his big red face soaked in sweat. Then Franklin appeared in his size twelve shoes, slogging through the mud.

Cole slumped against a tree, placing a hand on his chest. 'Give me five minutes, I need to catch my breath.'

Franklin shook his head. 'This is ridiculous. Why did we follow her here? We should have driven around for a bit, waited for her to come out.'

Franklin cupped his hands around his mouth. 'Jernegan,' he shouted. 'Jernegan, just give us the money. We'll tell Swain you got away, that we couldn't find you.' He stared up at the rock and, for a moment, Jernegan was sure he'd seen her. But the big man turned round, shaking his head at the trees.

Jernegan sighted down the barrel, aiming the gun at Franklin's head. She squeezed the trigger, the gunshot echoing through the woods. Franklin and Cole dived to the ground, covering their heads with their hands. Jernegan fired another shot, then another, her hands trembling. The magazine held fifteen rounds; surely, she was bound to hit something? She caught glimpses of them through the trees, crawling across the mud. She kept firing, aiming at the slightest sound, then stopped, breathing harder now, desperate to get her bearings.

Jernegan could hear her heartbeat thumping against the silence.

'Stop shooting, for God's sake,' Cole shouted. 'Just let us get out of these woods.'

'Sure,' Jernegan said, 'and what will you tell Swain?'

'Just like Franklin said, that we couldn't find you.'

'I can't do that.'

'Why not?'

'Like you said this morning, Cole, we've got unfinished business.'

'That was just a figure of speech. This is between you and Swain.'

Jernigan sighed. 'Why didn't he come himself?'

'Who knows? We're just the errand boys. You know that; it's nothing personal.'

'Is that right? Then ask Franklin about Connie's *accident*.'

Franklin and Cole remained silent. Then Jernegan saw something shuffling down the bank. She fired a shot into the air, noticing the darkening sky. As though he were a giant rising from the earth, Franklin stood up. He lifted his hands above his head. 'Take it easy now.'

'Stay still,' Jernegan shouted. 'Stay still or I'll shoot.'

Franklin froze. 'You're no killer, Jernegan. It's easy firing at trees. But you would have shot me by now. Only the frightened give you a warning.'

Jernegan squeezed the trigger and as the gun jammed, Franklin ran towards her. 'Cole,' he shouted, 'climb from the left, and hurry up.'

'It's too steep for me,' Cole shouted back. 'You know what I'm like with heights.'

Franklin sighed. 'Then don't look down.'

As the two men climbed, Jernegan pulled desperately on the trigger. 'Piece of shit,' she cursed, her temper worsening as the trapped shell refused to budge. Then she became conscious of Cole's voice, like a child, crying out for help.

'Franklin,' Cole kept saying. 'Franklin, you need to help me.'

Franklin kept climbing, only looking back when Cole's voice grew more desperate. The big man sighed. 'What's wrong now?'

'I've leaned too far out,' Cole said. 'It's too flat; there's nothing to hold on to.'

Jernegan peered over the edge, seeing Cole's face, thinking how she'd never seen a man look so afraid.

Cole's eyes were shut tight. 'Please, someone, help me.'

'Just hold on with one hand,' Franklin said. 'Then try to turn around and pull yourself back to the edge.'

'I can't. Please, Franklin, please, you need to help me.'

Franklin sighed. 'We don't have time for this. If you can't climb, then jump.'

For a moment, Cole remained still, his body held between the sky and the land, then he let go, his body falling backwards. Cole's scream resounded through the woods, the eerie cry of his life's last protest. Then there was silence, and his body lay face down, his blood seeping onto the grass.

JERNEGAN SHOVED the gun into her pocket and threw on her rucksack. She scrambled over the fence, running as fast as she could. She kept moving, gun shots barking behind her.

Her lungs felt ready to burst; a stitch stabbed at her side; her legs were on the brink of collapse. Only the thought of Connie kept her going, the murmur of her voice, like a need for survival, urging her forward.

When she reached the brow of the hill, she saw the lake glinting in the half-light. So far, the land had protected her, and she wondered if the darkness, too, might also prove to be her saviour. She heard Franklin getting closer, and each short pant for breath hounded her like a wolf. But fear did not overcome her, instead she felt a sense of belonging and an immediate connection with the land. She remembered it so clearly, years ago, when she played in these hills as a girl. Even back then she felt part of it, invisible almost, drifting like the wind through the trees.

Something roared in her ears, followed by a sharp pain tearing at her shoulder. She tumbled down the hill, then lay in the heather, the stones cutting into her back. She tried to stand, but the harder she tried, the more her body felt weighted.

The wind blew fiercer, each sudden gust raging against the darkness.

Jernegan cried out, but no one was there to answer.

Somehow, she moved her right arm, and by pressing her palm into the soil, she slowly pushed herself up. She staggered forward, the taste of metal lingering inside her mouth.

When she reached the bottom of the valley, the wind carried the call of her name. The voice sounded familiar, threatening, and triumphant.

She turned around, seeing Franklin's silhouette standing on the brow of the hill. The big man pointed his gun at her, pausing as though expecting her to run.

Instead, she shrugged off her rucksack, took a few steps forward, and slumped against a rock. Then she looked towards the horizon, watching the faint outline of Franklin's shape zigzagging towards her.

Darkness masked Franklin's face and a bloodless moon cast his shadow.

Jernegan stood up, tried to say something, but struggled to get her words out. She watched as Franklin picked up his pace. The big man trampled through the heather, as fast as the land allowed.

'Seen sense at last,' Franklin said. 'Accepted what's coming to you, nothing but whores, the pair of you.'

Jernegan remained silent. She started walking towards the path, slowly, waiting for that last bullet to drop her into the grass. All she heard was something scraping across the soil, followed by a brief clattering of stones and what sounded like a sharp cry for help.

When Jernegan turned round, she saw Franklin lying on his back. For a moment, she thought it was a trap. But there was no need for games. Franklin had caught her, the open land providing him with a clear shot.

The big man lay in the heather. Prickly thorns twisted around his arms and legs, as though he were vermin ensnared by the land. 'I slipped, fell arse over tit. Can you believe it?'

Jernegan stepped forward, watching as Franklin tried to sit up.

'You need to help me, Jernegan. My legs feel dead. I've got this pain shooting right down my back.'

Jernegan shrugged. 'What do you expect me to do?'

'Find someone, at least. Call for an ambulance.'

Jernegan forced a laugh, falling silent as she noticed the blood on her shoulder. 'Two minutes ago, you were trying to kill me.'

'Business, I only tried to wound you. Swain told us to

fetch you back.'

'Is that right? What about Connie? What was that, *personal*?'

'I was following orders. It a job. I . . . I didn't know she was with you.'

Jernegan rested on her haunches, then searched Franklin's pockets for his gun.

The big man looked up at her, his eyes shining. 'Please, I'm begging you. You don't need to do this.'

Jernegan breathed deeply and gazed across the lake. The moon shone brightly, reflecting across the water. With the clouds broken, the sky looked different, silvery almost, streaks of dark and pale blue blending as they caught the light. She looked up at the clouds and at the faces she saw within them. What would Connie think of all this, she wondered. But she was gone. Jernegan knew that, and their time together felt almost dreamlike. But the sky was real, as was the cold, the dark, and the night's silence.

Jernegan closed her eyes, the day's events returning to her in flashes. In her mind's eye, she saw the town, the moors, and the trees. Cole's body sprawled across the rocks. The strangeness of it all disturbed her. But she felt part of something, cared for, almost as though she were blessed. She opened her eyes, knowing the land had protected her, and now it wanted something back.

She pointed the gun at Franklin. 'This is for Connie,' she whispered.

Franklin tried to stand, but the harder he pushed, the more his body refused to budge. 'It doesn't have to be like this,' he said, his eyes glistening, sweat trickling down his face and neck.

Jernegan squeezed the trigger. 'You don't have any choice; the land has already decided.'

THE DARKNESS AND THE LIGHT

Billy was the runt of the litter. There was no denying it. He was the kid they shoved around. The guy they picked a fight with. He longed to be popular, but he just didn't have the face for it. He knew that. But it never stopped him from dreaming. Somewhere deep, a voice told him everything was possible.

Tonight, was his time to shine.

The warmest feeling, as if everything was about to change.

Even Degsy greeted him with a smile, his eyes shining as he slapped little Billy on the back. 'You always remind me of when we were kids, Billy. That gang we used to have, drinking all night, watching the sunrise every morning.'

Even back then, Billy didn't fit in, always screwing things up, always running out of chances. But Degsy was sweet on Billy's sister and always cut Billy some slack.

Degsy took hold of Billy's arm, sighing as he gazed out of the window. 'Who would have thought it. That we'd come this far, running the eastside of the bay.'

But Billy preferred the old days, selling uppers and

downers, eighths of weed, whiz when they could get their hands on it. He felt safer back then. He was one of the boys, striding behind Degsy's shadow.

'Don't look so worried,' Degsy said. 'Relax.'

Billy sat down, slumping into the chair.

Degsy smiled. 'Skinny Billy Briers. You always were the sensitive type, ever since we were kids. Do you remember that bird we found? Half dead, it was, twitching like a runt in the sand.'

Billy's eyes widened. 'I'll never forget it. The boys were going to toss it like a rag.'

'That's right, Billy. Until you picked it up, nursing it back to life, cradling it like a baby in your arms. That's why this job needs your touch. Someone quiet. Someone who won't react to Falon's mouth.'

Billy's heart thumped. He couldn't stop smiling. 'Are we actually gonna pay the bastard?'

Degsy stared at his hands. 'I don't see how we have any choice. We took down one of his boys. A mistake, I know. But the Boss says we need to put it right.'

'I understand,' Billy said.

Degsy picked up the package from his desk and threw it into Billy's lap.

Billy stood up. 'I won't let you down, Degsy. Not this time.'

Degsy looked away. 'I know that,' he said, his voice softening. 'And believe me, there'll be better jobs. We've just gotta take the darkness with the light.'

As HE HURRIED along the promenade, Billy kept those words in his head, whispering them over and over.

'Hey, it's Billy Runt,' the young kids shouted.

But Billy kept walking, smiling as he turned his collar to the cold.

Billy rarely ventured into town. He hated the noise and loathed the narrow confines of its streets. A siren blared. A myriad of lights flickered like stars in the distance. But Billy kept walking. Checking his pockets every five seconds, making sure nothing was lost.

He could smell the crack house from the far side of the road, tainting the air like poison. Music boomed through the windows, a reverberating bass pumping like a giant heart.

When he got to the end of the path, Billy found the door open. He stepped inside, the music deafening. To his surprise, Falon was already waiting, his hair slicked back, grinning from the foot of the stairs.

'He sent you after all,' Falon said. 'You've got to hand it to Degsy. He always lets his head rule his heart.'

Billy had no idea what Falon was talking about, so he chucked the package on the floor.

Falon kicked it open, laughing to himself as Billy gawped at the blank sheets of paper.

Then Falon pulled out his gun, the barrel's cold steel pressing into Billy's mouth.

'It's nothing personal,' Falon said. 'It's just what me and Degsy agreed, one of his for one of mine. If it makes things any better, Degsy felt bad about it. But shit happens, Billy. You've just got to take the darkness with the light.'

THE DEVILFISH

Louisa had been acting strange for a while. She started getting confused. One minute she was surviving the present, the next she was lost in the past. She kept forgetting things too, what day it was, where she was going, the names of people and places.

Most days she asked for her husband. She spent hours searching for him. Then grow tearful when they reminded her he'd passed away. The doctors warned her it would come, dementia. They told her it would be a gradual decline.

'I'm not going to any home,' she said. 'I'm too old to move. I've lived in this house all my life. I'll die in the place where I was born.'

She spent most of her days alone, her mind wandering in and out of time as a ghost. At night, she dreamed of the Devilfish. Chameleon-like and cunning, the creature lurked beneath the grey-blue waters of the River Dee. The voices in her head told her the creature was important. From years ago, she guessed, but couldn't remember why.

In her dreams, the creature watched her, two calm,

knowing eyes peering from the confines of a burrow. Then the water darkened, and a bulbous head emerged slowly out of the shadows.

The creature's skin was the colour of dust, mottled with brown and grey, like a devil born out of ashes. Its tentacles rose from their bed of shingles, swaying, sliding, and feeling their way through the water.

She watched it float above the rocks, snapping at anything that crossed its path. Then, as in every dream, it caught sight of her, its pale skin morphing to a dull red.

As it swam towards her, all Louisa could do was stare, mesmerised, listening to four hearts thumping against the silence. When its tentacles slithered across her skin, she'd wake up. Find herself lying in a wet bed, hoping to God that one of those hearts was her own.

For weeks now, Claire, the woman who claimed to be her daughter, kept calling at Louisa's house. Claire cooked for her, dusted, changed her sheets, washed and ironed her clothes. That morning, Claire arrived early. She brought the stranger with her, too. The man was pale and lanky, a weasel-faced runt with long, greasy hair.

Louisa could never remember his name. All she knew was that she didn't like him. If she remembered, she wouldn't have let him in. She would have known that he was nothing but trouble. A lying, worthless bum, who for years made her daughter's life hell.

The three of them sat at the kitchen table, drinking tea. Louisa stared into her mug, breathing in the hot steam. Then she looked up at her daughter. 'What the hell are you still doing here, anyway? You're going to be late, girl. You need to get yourself to school.'

Claire placed a hand on Louisa's shoulder. 'I'm not in school anymore, Mum. I'm almost forty.'

The stranger sniggered, causing Louisa to cast him a glance. 'And who's he? What the hell is he doing in my house?'

Claire smoothed her hand down Louisa's arm. 'This is my husband, Mum. Tony. Remember? I've told you a dozen times. We're back together now, giving it another go.'

Louisa sucked the air through her teeth, then stared at the five blue dots tattooed on Tony's left hand. 'Only ex-cons have those marks,' she said. 'This man's a wrong 'un if you ask me.'

Tony moved his hands from the table. 'I won't deny it. I've made mistakes, but I've also served my time.' He looked over at Claire. 'Jesus is in my life now. And with Claire's help, I'm hoping to make a fresh start.'

Louisa belched into her fist. 'That might be so. But it still doesn't explain what you're doing here.'

Tony opened his mouth to say something, but the look on Claire's face held him silent. Claire sighed into her hands. 'He's here to take you shopping, Mum. I'm doing a double shift today, remember?'

Louisa took a swig of tea, then banged her mug down on the table. 'I haven't got time to go shopping. I need to go down to the estuary, fix my stepfather's nets.'

Claire breathed deeply, then twiddled the ring on her finger. 'We've talked about this before. It's not safe for you down there. You're not a girl anymore. You stopped working there before I was born.'

Louisa shook her head. 'Don't talk daft. It's peak season. We fish for salmon until August.'

'No, Mum, not anymore. That's all gone now. Today, you're going shopping with Tony.'

. . .

LOUISA SAT in the back of Tony's car, trying to unfasten her seatbelt. She gazed through the window, squinting against the morning light. Seabirds flew across the skyline, white flecks fading into the endless blue.

Each time she closed her eyes, the Devilfish returned to her in flashes. She saw its bloodless skin, then the clouds of black ink ejecting from its gut. Jets of water spewed from its gills, projecting the creature forward. She knew it by another name, but no matter how hard she tried, she couldn't remember what. There was something bad about it too, something to do with her stepfather.

'We need to take the coast road,' she said. 'My stepfather doesn't like to be kept waiting. He has a mean temper, so you hurry up. You need to drop me off at the docks.'

Tony glanced into the rearview mirror, his dark eyes smiling. 'We're going to the shops, so stop mythering you crazy old bitch.'

Louisa sighed. 'You shouldn't talk to me like that. I'm going to tell Claire what you said.'

Tony laughed. 'Sure, you will. If you remember.'

For a moment, that raucous laugh reminded her who Tony was. He was Seth Whitehall's boy, slovenly like his mum and an idiot like his dad. She remembered Tony getting sent down for breaking into Whiteley's store. The fool set off all the alarms after falling through the roof. She asked Claire why he'd done it. Claire shrugged; her eyes fixed on the carpet. 'I don't know, Mum. He gets these stupid ideas sometimes. They take hold of him. He doesn't think about the consequences. Just convinces himself it's the right thing to do.'

Louisa sighed. The memory fading as she closed her eyes.

When they pulled into the supermarket car park, Louisa refused to budge. 'I'll wait for you here. Give me a shout if you need me.'

Tony grabbed her arm. 'Don't play me like you play Claire. Just get out of the car.'

Louisa stayed put until the poke in her ribs persuaded her otherwise. Tony led her inside. Then grabbed hold of a trolley and made her push it down the aisle. 'You should be in a home,' he said. 'Help me and Claire out for once. Let us sell that shithole you call a house.'

Louisa looked him in the eye. 'You're gonna have to wait. You're not getting that place until I'm dead.'

'Hmm, that might happen sooner than you think.'

Louisa didn't answer. Instead, she began filling the trolley with anything that took her fancy. Tony picked up a box of beer and dumped it in the front. 'Don't give me that look. You can afford a few beers. Think of it as payment for my services.'

Louisa didn't say another word. She just let him jabber on, thinking how rank he looked in that filthy red jacket.

They shopped for another half an hour until Tony got bored. He grabbed hold of Louisa's arm and guided her to the tills. She tried her best to help, but only got in the way. With a can of baked beans in his hand, Tony pointed towards the window. 'Wait over there, where I can see you.'

Louisa did as she was told and went and leaned against the glass. She basked in a wedge of sunlight, staring at her own shadow. In her mind's eye, she saw the Devilfish scouring the waters for a mate. The creature gleamed with phosphorescence, became a phantom sun glowing in the river's darkness. It reminded her of the estuary, and she remembered what she had to do.

She sneaked outside, the fresh air rolling across her tongue. She trod carefully down the bank, took a left towards the old railway bridge, strolling beneath the arches onto the Greenfield Valley trail. She followed it through the woods, catching glimpses of the Mill Pool glinting through the trees. Familiar smells flooded her senses, the soil, the leaves, the wild garlic. One minute she accepted the gutted ruins of the old mills. Then she'd forget, get confused, wonder why they'd been left to rot.

When she reached the Abbey, the path forked into three lanes. She kept staring at them, wondering which one to take. She took a left, walking faster now, chasing the sound of laughter.

Three boys sat on the pool wall, skimming stones across the water.

'Which way is it to the old docks?' she said. 'I can't for the life of me remember.'

The boys turned around, their faces sunburned and brazen. 'Do you mean the Mostyn Docks?' one of them said.

Louisa shook her head. 'No, Greenfield. You know, the Cob.'

The boy pointed east. 'It's just over there.' He grinned at the boy next to him. 'Cross over at the lights, then take the Old Dock Road.'

Louisa smiled, then carried on walking, sensing someone behind her.

THE OLD DOCK Road looked changed; it was no longer the place she remembered. A metal fence stood on both sides of the road, the railings rusty and spiked. She gazed at the sewage works, catching its smell on the breeze. The concrete storage tanks looked misplaced against the far stretch of water, and the noontime silence spoiled by their eerie thrum.

She walked to the edge of the car park, then stopped to catch her breath. She took in the road bridge, the old sluice gates, and the flushing pool behind them. She crossed the road, turned left, stepping slowly down the muddy ramp.

When she reached the bottom of the ramp, Louisa caught sight of her reflection in the water. She was shocked by how old she looked. She looked so tired, ragged like her stepfather's boat. 'What the hell's it doing here?' she mumbled. 'How are they going to cast the nets?'

'Who the hell are you talking to?' said a voice behind her.

She turned around and saw the stranger. He was still wearing that filthy red jacket. His slicked back hair was looking oilier beneath the noonday sun. She studied him a moment. 'Where do I know you from?'

The man lit a cigarette. 'It's me, you stupid old bitch, Tony.'

She shook her head. 'No, sorry, but I can't place you.'

Tony took a drag on his cigarette, then blew the smoke into her face. 'What the hell are you doing down here? What are you up to?'

Louisa sighed. 'I thought that was obvious. I'm going cockling in my stepfather's boat.'

Tony laughed and glanced across the estuary. 'The tide's getting rough, the weather's changing.'

'Well, I'm going anyway. If I fall in and drown, so be it. Let the river take me.'

'I'll help you then,' he said, a gleam in his eyes, as though the cleverest idea suddenly flashed behind them.

.   .   .

THEY WADED out to the boat. Louisa climbed aboard, keeping it steady while Tony untied the line. Once Tony was in the boat, Louisa rowed towards the estuary, using the ebb tide to make her way downstream. Tony sat opposite her. He took off his jacket and lit another cigarette. Louisa didn't like the way he smiled. And that sly look in his eyes reminded her of her stepfather.

Her stepfather's family fished these waters for generations. The Powells: a crew made up from cousins, nephews, and uncles, trammelling for salmon, known throughout the county as the driftnetsmen of the Dee.

'Connah's Quay trammel nets,' Louisa said. 'That's what they used to call them. A bastard to fix, but definitely the most deadly.'

Tony threw his jacket at her. 'Shut up, you old witch. What the hell are you jabbering on about?'

Louisa closed her eyes and sighed, an easterly wind carrying her back in time.

She was standing on the mud flats, watching the tide rising, the sound of the water growing fiercer, just like the roar of her stepfather's laughter. The netsmen talked about the Devilfish for days, and there were at least three sightings. Louisa thought of nothing else. The creature distracted her throughout the day and haunted her at night.

From what the netsmen told her, she knew the Devilfish was like no other creature in these waters. It fed on men, women, and children, too. The creature knew no mercy. Its massive tentacles could pull a boat under, drag it out to sea, and hold it there for weeks. Only the lost knew its secrets, and only the cursed heard the murmur of their ghosts.

Then, from across the water, her stepfather called out to her. 'Devilfish, Devilfish. Come here, girl, quickly.'

At first, she just stood there, petrified, staring at the boat. Then she remembered the consequences of not doing what he asked, and it was like a huge hand pushing her forward. She waded through the water, the shifting sands almost dragging her under. Eventually, she climbed onto the boat, breathing deeply as she stared at the creature lurking beneath the nets. It kept trying to free itself, shuffling and scrambling, its skin covered with mud and sand. She thought how small it looked, its frightened eyes casting her a furtive glance.

Louisa reached out her hand, holding it still as the boat rocked in the water. She looked up at her stepfather, sickened by the slyness of his smile. 'Liar, this isn't the Devilfish. It's nothing but a small octopus.'

He leaned over and slapped her face. 'I've told you about that mouth of yours. I'm no liar, girl. Devilfish is what they used to call them.'

She wiped the tears from her eyes. 'But I thought...'

'I know what you thought. Everyone's been teasing you for weeks. You're nothing but an embarrassment.' He smoothed his hand over her thigh. 'You're only good for one thing.'

Louisa slapped his hand away, but he just looked at her and grinned. 'Just you wait 'til we get back,' he said. Then he nodded towards the nets. 'Now get rid of that wretched thing.'

'It's tangled,' she said. 'I don't want to hurt it. It'll bleed to death if I cut it free.'

'And you will if you don't get on with it. Now, come on, don't make me tell you again.'

She picked up the knife, then put it down again,

deciding to pull the tentacles free. She took hold of one, gently feeling it slither inside her hand.

Her stepfather sighed. 'Get on with it. We haven't got all day.'

Louisa cast him a glance, taking her time until he grabbed hold of her shoulders. She tried to shrug him off, almost breaking free. She hated his touch and that smell of stale alcohol breezing across her neck. She kept her back turned, pushing against him as he tried to lift her up. She pressed down with all her weight, hooking her feet into the nets and trying to use them as an anchor.

'It's time for a little swim,' he said. 'Don't struggle, there's no use in both of us getting wet.'

She cried out, growing more tired as he dragged her closer to the water. The current was strong, the highest waves sloshing onto the boat. With his hand on the back of her neck, he pushed her face into the water. She kept her eyes closed. The river's saltiness gushed through her nose and down her throat. She tried not to panic, even though his grip was firm, his strength impossible to resist. What a pathetic way to die, she thought. Her sadness was intensifying as her brief life flashed before her.

As one last act of defiance, she gripped hold of the boat. She pushed it with all her strength, trying desperately to rock it forward. For a moment, she thought she'd succeeded. The hand released her neck, and she lifted her head out of the water. She slumped onto her side, coughing and spluttering, tears coursing down her face.

He crouched over her and smiled. 'You're not dead yet. That was just a taster.'

She lay still for a moment, listening to the seabirds, until finally lifting herself up. She felt the cold wetness of her clothes, and a feeling of shame crept inside her.

'Just take us back,' he said. 'At least, do something useful for once.'

She grabbed an oar, holding it tight, her heart thumping as he sat in front of her. He gave her that look of his, and she fixed her eyes on his smile. Then, just as he was about to put his hand on her thigh, she jumped up and swung the oar into his face. He shouted something, then fell backwards, covering his face with his hands. Louisa struck him again. She kept ramming the oar into his face, watching him choke, listening to the blood gurgling inside his mouth. As he gasped his last breath, she crouched beside him. She watched the life fade from his eyes, feeling nothing as she pushed his body into the water.

Then she rowed out to sea, closing her eyes, wondering what the best thing would be to do.

WHEN LOUISA OPENED HER EYES, she had no idea where she was. What was she doing, a woman of her age, floating in the estuary on a boat?

There was no sign of the stranger, the man who drove her into town. A filthy red jacket lay at her feet, part of it smeared with blood. She glanced down at her hands, noticing there was blood on them too.

Louisa leaned forward, picked up a smouldering cigarette and put it in her mouth. She puffed on it a few times, then took a deep drag, coughing as she inhaled the smoke. She knew the Devilfish had something to do with all this, but, as always, she couldn't remember why. She gazed towards the shore, feeling empty inside. She felt robbed but wasn't sure of what.

YOUR FATHER'S SON

You break in through the back, just like your uncle Mikey showed you. But old Jonesy's gone out; recently it seems, owing to the cup of coffee steaming on the kitchen table. You decide to wait. Not that you have any choice. No. You have to make your name with this one.

You pull back a chair and sit down. The kitchen looks just like your mum's. Even smells the same, a recent mix of fried eggs and cigarettes. In fact, you half expect to see her standing at the sink, fussing over you, just like when you were a kid. Your dad hated that, insisted you needed toughening up, even tried to teach you boxing.

'It's no use,' he said. 'You've got your mother's softness.'

Those words cut you deep, so from then on you tried to be your father's son. Not that you saw him that much. Your uncle Mikey raised you. Your dad spent most of his time in jail.

. . .

YOU WANDER INTO THE LOUNGE, staring at the photographs on the mantel. Most of them are of Jonesy and his wife. Captured moments of time aligned chronologically. You pick one up and hold it to the light. Jonesy looks so young. His beautiful wife is by his side, her strawberry-blonde curls glowing like a summer fire.

You smile, and Mikey's words come flooding back to you: 'Old Jonesy's not the man he was, especially since his wife took ill. He's been nursing her for years. Dementia, or so I'm told. It's a sad state of affairs, but he owes Mr. Hale, and he's been telling folks he's paying no one. Jonesy knows the score; he collected enough debts in his day. You remind him. Make your old man proud.'

You wander back into the hall, thinking how pathetic it all is, the has-been versus the wannabe. You sound like your mum. But not your dad. No. Such thoughts would never have occurred to him. When you were twelve years old, you went to visit him in jail. You even drew him a picture, two men fighting in the street.

'Which one's me?' he asked.

You pointed to the larger of the two, the man with his shirt off.

He stared at it for a second. 'This is all wrong; I've told you before, keep your hands up; only a fool comes out swinging punches.'

YOU WANDER UPSTAIRS, following a pale creep of light. You open the door and see Jonesy's wife. She's lying on the bed, her eyes and mouth wide open. Her red satin nightie looks misplaced against her shrivelled skin. A relic of her past. A desperate hope. A failed reminder. Did she finally forget how to breathe? Did she take her last breath in limbo? You think how frail she looks, deflated, the life sucked out of her. It's not the first time you've been this close to death, and it reminds you of your dad.

You hear something, turn around, and see Jonesy by the door, clenching his liver-spotted hands. He staggers over to the bed, leans over his wife and kisses her forehead. He stays there awhile, making a whining sound, his big shoulders shaking.

You tell him you're here for him. That you found her like this. How it has nothing to do with you. Jonesy isn't listening and lunges towards you.

The old man's strong, and it takes all your strength to restrain him. You shove him against the wall, holding him until he calms down.

'I'm all right now,' he says, wheezing.

You let him go, watching as he puts his hands in his pockets and stares down at the carpet. The sadness in his eyes touches you. You tell him you'll come back another time, and that you'll make some excuse to Mikey.

Jonesy leans forward and says he knew your dad. 'You're nothing like him, though. No. He was the real deal. Mean.'

You smile, try to say something, but the knife in your throat holds you silent.

BILLY STAR

Mum always said that dad and his family were miscreants, but I never really knew what she meant until years later. A month before my thirteenth birthday, we left Liverpool and went to live with my nana in Wales. When I asked Dad why, he said, 'Because we've been evicted, and that whore mother of yours has left us.'

I didn't defend her, knowing he'd only shout me down.

Nana lived in northeast Wales, near the Dee estuary. It was the summer of the long drought, 1976.

I spent the first week thinking about Mum and gazing across the water. On clear days, you could see right across the Wirral shore and, sometimes, Liverpool shimmering beyond the haze.

I made friends with a boy my age called Luke and his older sister, Jodi. They gave me a tour of the town, told me who was who. As the weeks dragged on, we fell into a routine. We spent our mornings in a sleazy café called The Ritz. I was unsure whether the owners named the place as a joke. The tea was cheap, though, and they didn't seem to mind us hanging around. In the afternoons, we strolled down to the estuary, throw stones into the water, and when the tide was out, we'd see how far we could walk across the sands. We soon got bored with it, and those first few weeks seemed never-ending. Then Dad's younger brother came home, making it a summer the entire town would remember.

I FIRST MET BILLY one Saturday morning. I slept in late, woken by his raucous laughter. When I wandered into the kitchen, Billy leaned back into his chair, put his feet on the table and said, 'Look what the cat's dragged in.'

He was better looking than Dad, dressed a lot cooler too. He wore a faded denim shirt and flared jeans to match. He had blonde, shoulder-length hair, and the tiny gold star hanging from his left ear shone when it caught the light.

Nana placed a hand on my shoulder. 'Scott, this is your uncle Billy, why don't you say hello.'

I just nodded, not really knowing what else to say.

Billy smiled, took something from his back pocket and held it in his fist. 'Guess what I've got?'

I shrugged, more interested in the tattoos on his knuckles. He opened his hand, revealing a small silver coin. 'Do you know what it is?'

I shook my head.

'An American dime, my lucky charm, I brought it back from the States.'

'You've been to America?'

'Yeah, a few years ago, 'Frisco, New York, Pittsburgh Pennsylvania.'

'Meet anyone famous?'

'A few, shared a beer with Lee Majors once, the Six Million Dollar Man.'

'He's not really bionic, you know.'

'Shit, no way, and there's me thinking it's a documentary.'

I liked him from that moment on. He was the first person to make me laugh in weeks.

THAT MORNING, after Nana went to town, Billy told me about his travels. The fights he'd won. The women he'd left behind. I thought how hard it must have been for him. All the things he'd done, and here he was trapped in this one-street town, just like me. He slipped his hand down the back of his jeans and pulled out a gun. 'It's a .38 snubnose,' he said.

'Is it real?'

'Course it is, hold it if you like.'

I held it for a few seconds, then got scared and gave it back.

Billy winked. 'Don't say a word to your dad. This is between you and me.'

'Sure,' I said, sworn to keep his secrets. Then, just as I was about to ask Billy where he got it from, Dad walked in, causing Billy to sit up and take his feet off the table. Dad cast Billy a glance. 'I heard you were back.'

Billy grinned. 'Yep, it's been in all the papers. They even announced it on the radio.'

Dad got himself a beer from the fridge, took a few long swigs, and said, 'Still got that mouth on you, hey. So, what have you two been up to?'

'Just talking, trying to get to know my nephew.'

Dad shook his head and sighed. 'Don't go filling the boy's head with shit. He's already got a big imagination.'

I SPENT the next few days following Billy around. He didn't seem to mind, kept calling me his little shadow. We lay in the back garden, wearing nothing but shorts, baking beneath the sun. Sometimes I caught him staring at me, his eyes full of sadness. He said the strangest things, as though he knew what I was thinking. 'You better get used to this shithole, Scott. Your mum's not coming back, not if she's got any sense.'

I didn't speak for hours afterwards, kept my eyes fixed on the grass.

The things Billy said never bothered him. He didn't seem to care who got hurt. Whenever I told Nana about it, she defended him, then tell me to stop sulking. It was always the case. In her eyes, Billy could do no wrong. I could see why she thought that. I felt it too, but it still didn't make it right. She seemed happier when Billy was around, dressed nicer, always laughed at his jokes. 'When are you going to settle down?' she'd say. 'A handsome boy like you should give his mother a grand-child.' Then she'd look straight through me as if I wasn't there.

THE FOLLOWING SATURDAY, Luke came around. He looked lost, said he hadn't seen me for ages, wondered what I'd been up to?

'Nothing much,' I said.

He scraped the heel of his pump across the step. 'I saw some rats near the estuary, show you if you like?'

I didn't answer, and we just stared at each other for a while, caught in an awkward silence. As I wandered back inside, Billy blocked my way. 'What's all this about rats? You lads wait there. I'll fetch my old .22.'

We took a shortcut to the estuary through the valley woods. Billy walked between us with the rifle strapped across his shoulder. He didn't care if anyone saw him. Neither did I; it made me feel kind of reckless, closer to Dad, too.

As we walked, Billy asked Luke some questions. The usual stuff. How old was he? Did he have a girlfriend? What was he going to do when he left school? Luke didn't say much at first. He blushed a lot, thought too much about his answers. Billy soon charmed him, though, and after a while, you couldn't shut Luke up.

When we got to the old docks, we saw Jodi. She was sitting on the wall, listening to her transistor radio. She wore tight denim shorts and a yellow vest, her long, brown legs shining in the noonday sun. Billy put his fingers in his mouth and wolf-whistled, then said, 'Jesus, look at that.'

'Look at what?' Luke said.

'That stunning blonde over there.'

Jodi waved at us, and Billy waved back. He gave Luke a nudge. 'Do you know this girl?'

Luke frowned. 'Yeah, that's my sister Jodi.'

Billy shook his head. 'I'd never have guessed. Luckily for her, there's no similarity.' He placed a hand on Luke's shoulder. 'Come on then, introduce me.'

As we got closer, Jodi stood up and smoothed her hand over her hair. She was pretty, I suppose. But I never thought about her in that way. Self-protection, I guess. A seventeen-year-old girl would never be interested in me. She liked

Billy, though. I could tell that by her smile and the way she looked at him when he spoke.

Billy gave me the rifle, took some pellets out of his pocket and held them in his hand. 'Take 'em, should be enough to last you.'

He studied me for a moment. 'You know how to use it, right?'

'Sure, I've gone shooting with Dad loads of times.'

Billy smiled. 'Go and kill some rats then. Go on, the pair of you. I'll wait here with Jodi.'

I did as he said, not really knowing where to go. I followed the coastal path, Luke dragging his heels behind me. He kept mumbling and looking over his shoulder. I just ignored him and started walking faster, stopping when I reached the gate. While I waited for him to catch up, it felt strange standing there, stretches of fields on my left and the blue-grey river on my right. I had no attachment to the place. I felt lost, those wide, open spaces giving me the saddest feeling.

As Luke stood in front of me, he asked me what was wrong. I stared into his moody face. 'That's what I was just about to ask you.'

'I'm fine, just thinking.'

'About what?'

'Forget it.'

'No, go on.'

He looked down at the grass. 'How old's your uncle?'

'Not that old, eighteen or nineteen at the most.'

Luke shook his head. 'Looks in his twenties to me.'

'Twenty-one then, why d'you care?'

He held my stare for a moment, then looked across the fields. 'We're going the wrong way. The rats are near the rocks.'

When he started walking back, I called after him. He didn't turn around, just gestured for me to follow. I slung the rifle over my shoulder, thinking I'd have been better off staying at home.

We found Jodi sitting with Billy on the rocks, her arm around his waist, resting her head on his shoulder. They were singing along to the radio, Dolly Parton's 'Jolene'. Billy kept changing the words, replacing Jolene with Jodi, singing 'I'm begging you, please let me be your man.'

WE SPENT the next few days at the estuary, Luke and I wandering around the old docks while Billy spent his time with Jodi. Whenever I looked back, Billy had his arm around her, making her laugh and whispering into her ear. Sometimes they went for a walk, stopping before they reached the trees, settling into the long grass. Luke always asked if he could come, but Jodi told him never to follow. She seemed different now. She started wearing makeup, changed her hairstyle, which made her look older. That shy, considerate girl had disappeared, replaced by someone colder. It didn't bother me. It affected Luke the most. He'd compete for her attention, contradicting everything Billy said. Yet Billy was too quick for him, always putting him down.

ONE AFTERNOON, the four of us were sitting on the rocks, watching the shore glinting beneath the sun. Billy shielded his eyes against the light and pointed to the distant stretch of land. 'You can drive all the way to the other side when the tide's out.'

'How d'you know?' I said.

'Done it, years ago, borrowed a friend's Land Rover, drove right across the sands.'

'Bullshit,' Luke said. 'No way, and who do you know that has a Land Rover?'

Luke's sudden outburst surprised us all, but Billy seemed shocked by it the most. I thought Billy was going to slap him. From what he told me, he'd beaten people up for less. He just smiled, shook his head and rested a hand on Luke's shoulder. 'You need to calm down, Luke. Jodi told me what happens when you get upset; I don't want you pissing the bed.'

Luke stood up and glared at Jodi, his eyes shining. 'I'm going to tell Dad about you and him.' He sniffed back a tear. 'I hate you, Jodi. What did you tell him that for?'

When Luke started walking towards the road, Jodi tried to follow. Billy grabbed her arm, forcing her to stay put. 'Let him go. If he's gonna give it out, he needs to learn to take it.'

We didn't talk about it after that. We just sat on the rocks, listening to Jodi singing along to the radio.

THE FOLLOWING TUESDAY, I spent the entire morning watching the street from my bedroom window. I was waiting for Billy's friend, Dave. He was a bricklayer, taking us to one of his jobs and paying us for a day's work. I pestered Dad for weeks to get me a job. 'I'll see what I can do,' he said, but when I asked Billy, he arranged it the same day. He told me the night before. 'Dave owed me a favour,' he said, 'so I called it in.'

By midday, there was no sign of Dave. When I asked Billy if he was still coming, he told me to relax and wait. 'He's probably on another job. He'll be here before one.'

Dad laughed when he heard this. 'Sure, he will, that's if Dave exists.'

Billy glared at him. 'Why would I lie?'

'I've no idea, but lying's what you do.'

Billy sighed. 'Why are you always at me?'

'Because I know what you're like. I warned you; don't go filling the lad's head with your stories.'

'I'm not telling stories. Dave said he'd be here this morning.'

'Dave who?'

Billy paused. 'Dave J... Dave Jacobs.'

Dad laughed again. 'You know, the sad thing is I think you actually convince yourself this shit is true.'

Billy clenched his fists. 'You need to watch your mouth.'

Dad walked over to him. 'Or you'll do what exactly?'

Billy didn't say a word, just stormed out. I tried to chase after him, but Dad grabbed my arm. He stared at me for a second, and the tenderness in his eyes surprised me. His breath stank of beer, the smell growing stronger as I pleaded for him to let me go. He loosened his grip, almost causing me to fall over.

'I'll be back later,' I said, pausing when I reached the door. I turned to face him. 'It's not Billy's fault if Dave let him down. He's only trying to help me. There's no need to be jealous of him, you know.'

Dad shook his head and smiled, then told me to take care.

BILLY HAD REACHED the estuary when I caught up with him. His fists clenched, cursing under his breath. I wanted to ask if he was okay but guessed it would only make things worse.

He didn't say a word until we spotted Jodi. She was waiting at the old docks, sitting on an upturned boat. Two boys stood by her, smoking cigarettes.

'Who the hell are they?' Billy said.

I shrugged. 'Friends from school, I guess.'

Billy handed me his jacket. 'Hold this a minute. Let's see what they're up to.'

I trailed behind him, breaking into a jog as he started walking faster. The boys went quiet when they saw him. Jodi looked nervous too. Billy grabbed her hand and pulled her towards him, then slipped his arm around her waist. He snatched one of the boy's cigarettes and put the lit end in his mouth, streams of smoke pouring through the filter. Then he handed it back. 'That's called shotgun,' he said, 'now you try.'

The boy shook his head.

Billy grinned. 'What's wrong blow-wave, afraid you might burn your hair?'

As the other boy stepped forward, I couldn't keep my eyes off his t-shirt; it was a picture of Kung Fu, walking bare-foot across the sands.

Billy stared into the boy's eyes. 'What about you, Kwai Chang Caine? Why don't you try?'

The boy took his cigarette out of his mouth and flicked it across the path. 'Nah, not me. Seems like a stupid thing to do.' He glanced at his friend and smiled, then said, 'and the name's Mikey by the way.'

Billy took his hand from Jodi's waist. 'Is that right? Mikey who?'

'Mikey Rowlands,' she said. 'He's Shane Rowlands' younger brother.'

Billy shrugged. 'So, is that supposed to mean something? I've never heard of either of them.'

Mikey motioned towards the path, but Billy blocked his way. 'Where do you think you're going? You owe me an apology.'

'For what?'

'Mouthing off, coming on to my girl.'

Jodi grabbed Billy's hand. 'Leave him alone. We were just talking. I've known Mikey for years; he's a family friend. Shane works for my dad.'

Billy poked Mikey's chest. 'If he's known you so long, then he needs to show more respect.'

I stood and watched, waiting for that Billy Star smile. Billy only fought men. These were just boys, a few years older than me. I knew any second now Billy would start laughing, tell us it was all a joke. But Billy kept on at him, poking and prodding until the tears welled in Mikey's eyes.

I HARDLY SAW Billy after that, just caught glimpses of him flitting in and out of the house. He never said much; it was almost as though he was avoiding me. The day before my thirteenth birthday, Nana told me to invite Luke to my birthday tea. I hadn't seen him in ages, not since that time at the estuary. When I called at his house, his dad said he'd gone out. 'He's gone off on his bike somewhere,' he said, then asked if I'd seen Jodi.

I saw Luke twenty minutes later, pushing his bike up Moor Hill. I shouted his name a few times, and at first, he pretended not to hear me. When he turned around, I told him to wait for me at the top, and as we walked towards town, I asked if he was okay.

'Not bad,' he said.

'Why haven't you been down to the estuary?'

'You know why.'

'Because of Billy, you're still angry?'

He nodded. 'With good reason too.'

'He was just having a laugh. You started it. Why do you hate him so much?'

'Because he's too old for Jodi for a start. Anyway, it's not just me. Half the town thinks he's a prick. Dad won't have him near the house.'

'Nobody thinks he's a prick. What the hell do you know?'

'I know he's never been to America.'

'Then where did he get his snubnose?'

'Another convict, I suppose. Dad said he just got out of jail.' Luke threw me a glance. '*Snubnose*... I bet it's not even real.'

'It is too. Anyway, I bet your dad's lying; he's just trying to turn Jodi against him.'

'Billy's the liar. He's always bullshitting. Everyone around here thinks he's a joke. That's why they call him Billy Star.'

'They call him Billy Star because of his earring.'

Luke smiled. 'Yeah, right. If you don't believe me, then ask him.'

THAT NIGHT, Billy came home drunk. He brought me a bag of chips and asked if I fancied talking. He jabbered on like a machine gun. 'Things are on the up,' he said, 'especially since I met Jodi. That girl's gonna be famous one day. Top twenty, I reckon, sings like an angel.'

I mulled it over as I sucked the vinegar off my fingers. 'She has a pleasant voice, I suppose. But she's gonna have to wait.'

Billy snatched the chips from my hand. 'Why?'

'She needs to finish her A-levels; that's one more year of school.'

He handed me the bag, then lit a cigarette. He took a deep drag, blowing the smoke up at the ceiling. 'She's not doing her 'A' levels, she's coming to London with me.'

'London?'

'Yeah, I've got a job lined up. A guy I know has his own recording studio. It's a surprise, so don't you say a thing.'

I didn't answer, keeping quiet until Billy asked me what was wrong.

'Nothing.'

'Cheer up, then. Tomorrow's your birthday. I've got a special day planned. I'm gonna drive you across the sands, then take you to my favourite pub.'

I sat up, beaming, hoping it was all true. 'Whose car are you using? What if the pub won't serve me?'

'Just simmer down. Get some rest. Leave the details to me.'

I lay back and closed my eyes, but no matter how hard I tried, I couldn't sleep. The night was so quiet, and you could hear the rumble of the trains in the distance. I knew what Luke said wasn't true, but I still couldn't stop myself from asking. 'Billy?'

'Yeah'

'Why do they call you Billy Star?'

He didn't answer for a while, then said, 'because I'm a bright light, shining in the darkness.'

WHEN I WOKE the next morning, Billy was already up. I pulled on some clothes and went downstairs, expecting to see him in his chair. The house was empty, and as I wandered into the kitchen, I found three unopened cards lying flat on the table. The first card I opened was from Dad, a cheap one from the market, a pastel drawing of a boat. He'd written ALL THE BEST inside and given me a crumpled fiver. Nana's card looked almost the same, but she only gave me a quid. Mum's card was the biggest. It had my name and address on the envelope written in blue ink. It was a nice card too, a picture of a red Ferrari. I thought she would have written me a note, explaining why she left. But all she put was Love Mum P.S. I miss you. She sent me twenty quid, though, a fortune back then, and I kept bragging about it to Nana and Dad the moment they came in.

Nana insisted I give it to her. 'I'll look after it for you. It's a lot for a boy of your age to be carrying around.'

I didn't answer her, turning away when she said, 'don't look at me like that; I'll give it you back as soon as you see something you want.'

Before handing it over, I made a mark on it with a blue Biro, so I'd know which one it was.

Nana didn't like that. 'This boy's just like his mother, but where is she today, hey? If it were left to her, he'd have no party.'

Dad sighed. 'Scott meant no harm. Let's not ruin his day.'

Nana put the twenty in her purse and snapped it shut. 'You should have seen the look he gave me. It's your fault for spoiling him.'

Dad forced a laugh. 'You're a fine one to talk.'

'What do you mean?'

'You spoiled Billy rotten. That's why he's like he is.'

'There's nothing wrong with him; just you leave him alone. You're always going on at him.'

'And why's that I wonder?'

They carried on like this for a while, Dad getting more frustrated, Nana refusing to let it go. I grew tired of it in the end and sloped off into the garden. I spent a few hours there, swinging back and forth on the gate, waiting for Billy to show.

About 4.30 Nana called me in for tea. My birthday spread as Dad called it, nothing more than a few bowls of crisps, a half-set jelly, and a pile of beef paste sandwiches. At least they bought me a cake, a jam sponge with thirteen candles. I tried my best to tuck in, didn't want to seem ungrateful. I ate some crisps, chewed the middle from a sandwich.

Nana shook her head. 'I don't know why I bothered; you pair haven't touched a thing.'

We didn't answer. Then Dad flicked open his lighter and lit the candles. 'Blow them out in one, Scott. Then make a wish but keep it to yourself.'

I wished for Mum to come and fetch me, but as Billy came strolling into the house, I settled for the next best thing.

Billy rested his hands on Nana's shoulders, kissed her cheek. She placed a hand on his, smiling as she squeezed his fingers. Deep down, I knew he'd come. No matter what Luke or Dad said about him, I knew he wouldn't let me down. He walked over to me and ruffled my hair, then started singing Happy Birthday. He sang it in a strange, high-pitched voice, which even made Dad smile.

Nana laughed the loudest. 'Thank God you're here. Now it feels like a party.'

Billy grabbed some crisps. 'I wouldn't miss this for the world; Scott's my favourite nephew.'

'You've got him something special then,' Dad said,

'saving it till now, because I didn't see your card on the table.'

'Shit,' Billy said. 'I knew there was something.' He looked at me and smiled. 'Sorry, Bud. My head's all over the place. I've gone and left your present in my mate's.'

Dad scraped back his chair, shook his head, and went outside for a smoke.

'That's all right,' I said.

Nana smiled. 'Course it is, Billy will give it to you in the morning.'

She started clearing the table, then Billy said, 'Mum, I really need to speak with you.'

Nana froze and gripped the paper plate. 'Why? What's happened now, Billy?'

'Nothing, just need to tell you something that's all.'

She walked over to the sink, and with her back turned said, 'you best tell me now. Scott, go outside and play.'

I did as I was told, leaving the door ajar. Dad sat on the steps, smoking a cigarette, staring into next door's garden. He turned to face me, flicked the ash from his clothes. 'You all right?'

I nodded and looked back into the house. Billy was standing with Nana at the sink. She was crying, and he had his hands on her shoulders. 'I know,' he said in a hushed voice. 'I won't let you down. This time, it'll be different.'

He stopped talking when he saw me. Then he whispered something into Nana's ear, causing her to turn around and slam the door.

'Jesus,' Dad said, 'what the hell's wrong with her now?'

I shrugged. 'Billy wanted to tell her something.'

Dad stubbed out his cigarette. 'Here we go again.'

Then Nana came outside, wiping her eyes as she asked Dad if she could have a word. I followed them into the house. There was no sign of Billy, and I asked Nana several times before she answered me.

'Will you stop mythering me, child. Billy's gone.' She broke into tears. 'God knows when he's coming back.'

I rushed outside, Dad calling after me. I didn't answer, just kept running, racing through the avenues, never once stopping for breath. I caught Billy up at the fire station. He turned around and waited for me by the wall. 'You're fast on your feet,' he said. 'For a moment, I thought it was Steve Austin.'

I didn't answer. I just stared at the sports bag slung over his shoulder.

Billy caught my glance. 'I was going to send you a post-card. I hate goodbyes, always get over emotional.'

'No worries, but we can still go to your favourite pub.'

Billy shook his head. 'I doubt if they'd serve you, another time perhaps. Listen, I've got to get going. I'm meeting Jodi at the station.'

'What about the Land Rover, I thought you were driving?'

Billy looked away. 'Nah, my contact let me down. Anyway, the train will be more fun.'

I nodded. 'Do you mind if I see you off?'

Billy laughed. 'It seems I don't have any choice.'

As we walked, Billy kept telling me to hurry up. 'Can't afford to be late, there isn't a direct train for hours after this one.'

I was going as fast as I could. He was being a bit harsh, considering it was my birthday. I grew angrier the more I thought about it, then told him I was heading back.

'See ya then,' he said, didn't even ask me what was wrong.

'Oh, and thanks for the drink by the way, and the present you got me for my birthday.'

Billy gave me a dirty look. Then, as he was about to say something, a tan Austin Maxi pulled up alongside us. I recognised Jodi's dad the moment he wound down the window. 'How's it going, Scott?'

'Fine thanks, Mr. Harrison.'

He looked really pissed off, so did the guy sat next to him.

They got out of the car and walked towards us.

Billy motioned towards the kerb, and Mr. Harrison blocked his way. 'Hey, Billy, where you off to?'

Billy grinned. 'That's my business.'

'Don't be smart,' the other guy said. 'Mr. Harrison asked you a question.'

Billy shifted the strap on his shoulder. 'And I answered him. Anyway, I'll be as smart as I like. Who the hell are you?'

'I'm Shane Rowlands. I believe you've already met my younger brother Mikey.'

Mr. Harrison grabbed Shane's arm. 'Thing is, Billy, you're old enough to be as smart as you like. But that doesn't apply to Jodi.'

Billy lifted the bag from his shoulder and dropped it on the pavement. 'Jodi's *seventeen*. You make her sound like a baby.'

'She still is to her mum and me. That's why she isn't going to London.'

Billy sucked the air through his teeth. 'You should let her make up her own mind.'

Mr. Harrison's jaw tightened. 'I will, after her exams, when she's finished her degree.'

Billy sighed. 'Let's see what Jodi has to say about it.'

Mr. Harrison shook his head. 'No, Billy. You can't see her anymore, just keep away.'

'Yeah right, just you try to stop me.'

Mr. Harrison stepped aside, allowing Shane through. Shane was tall and broad, almost as big as Dad. When he pressed his forehead into the bridge of Billy's nose, I thought Billy would go crazy. But he didn't do a thing, and when Shane stared into his eyes, Billy just looked away.

Shane grabbed Billy's shirt. 'You bullshitting little prick. You're a joke, picking on kids, stealing their cigarettes. Just do as you're told and keep away from Jodi.' He slapped Billy's face. 'Answer me then.'

Billy nodded.

Shane slapped him again. 'Now tell me you're a little shit, and you'll keep away from Jodi.'

'I'm a little shit,' Billy said, his voice trembling.

'And?'

'I'll keep away from Jodi.'

Shane let go of Billy's shirt and shoved him against the hedge. He kept staring at Billy as he walked back to the car, still watching him as they drove away.

When Billy grabbed his bag and turned around, I started walking alongside him. We didn't speak for ages, and just before we reached town, Billy took a left down a side street. He stopped and lit a cigarette, his hand shaking. He took deep drags, cursing as he breathed out the smoke. 'Wanker. I'll show him.'

Tears welled in Billy's eyes, so I asked if he was okay.

'I'm fine, just angry.' He flicked his cigarette across the road. 'I wasn't scared of him you know, just played along with it. I was gonna knock the prick out. But I've got to be careful, one more slip I'd be back inside. I'm still on probation.' He stared at me for a moment. 'Don't tell anyone about this.'

I nodded.

'Good, lad, I know you can keep a secret.'

'What we gonna do now?'

'We're doing nothing. You're going home, and I'm going for a drink.'

A STRANGE THING happened to me that night. Half an hour before the police came, I woke up. I felt empty inside; it was the saddest feeling. I climbed over to Billy's bed and stuck my head out of the window. The air was warm. An amber lit haze shone in the nighttime sky. I heard the rush of traffic. A dog barked. Then sirens blared in the distance. It seemed to come from the estuary, and when I looked towards the sands, I saw glimpses of blue flashing lights. Then a police car pulled up in front of the house. My heart thumping as they hammered on the door.

The doctor gave Nana Valium that night. The news about Billy was too much for her. After the police left, Dad stood by the front door drinking. He kept looking at me over his shoulder, his sad eyes glistening.

We didn't sleep that night. In fact, we hardly slept for weeks.

The news about Billy was all over town. People spoke about nothing else, especially after his and Jodi's funeral. Billy was drunk, or so they said, when he knocked on Shane Rowlands's door and shot him in the head. They said he forced Jodi to come with him, steal her Dad's keys, but I knew that wasn't true. They said he was driving over 90 mph before he lost control of the car and flipped it over the rocks. Most wondered what he was doing there. Only I knew the truth. He tried to beat the tide and drive across those endless sands. I said nothing, even when the police questioned me.

'Is there anything you can tell us, Scott?' they said. 'Did he say anything to you that night?'

But I just shook my head, and just like I promised Billy, I never said a thing.

THANKS FOR READING

Thanks for reading. If you **enjoyed this book,** please consider leaving **a review.** Reviews make a huge difference in helping new readers find the book.

WELCOME TO HOLYHELL

'Welcome To HolyHell has the sharp plotting of peak Elmore Leonard combined with the brooding lyrical atmosphere of James Lee Burke. The characters are all marvelously well-drawn and the sense of time and place is spot on.' *Punk Noir Magazine*

'Math Bird gives us a fine bit of noir in 1976 Wales.' *Murder in Common Crime Fiction Blog*

'A remarkable work that will have you dreading as well as eagerly turning the page.' *Unlawful Acts - Crime Fiction blog*

Lies...

It's 1976, and Britain is in the grip of an unbearable heatwave when conman Bowen flees London to return to his hometown, hoping for a fresh start ... but things don't always go according to plan.

Secrets...

For young loner, Jay Ellis finding a briefcase full of cash seems the answer to all his prayers, as does the magnetic pull of the stranger, Nash, who rolls into town shortly after.

Betrayal...

Veteran conman Nash is hot on Bowen's trail to find the money stolen from him. All he has is a hunch and a newspaper clipping of the boy who witnessed his partner's death. Their fates become entwined, but in a world of violent drifters and treacherous thieves, a man's conscience can become his weakness.

A compelling, poignant and dark thriller, rich with atmosphere, for fans of small-town crime and rural noir.

Welcome to Holyhell **... where secrets can prove deadly**

HIDDEN GRACE

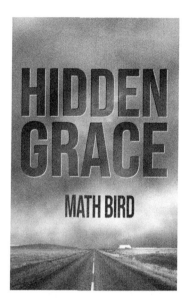

Only revenge can bury the sins of the past, but are the hunters about to become the prey...

Ned Flynn's days are haunted by those who betrayed him, and payback seems the only road to forgiveness. Yet Flynn doesn't know where to start until retired criminal Eddie Roscoe throws him a lifeline.

But Eddie's services come with a price, and if Flynn wants the information he seeks, he must help a distraught Eddie find his missing son.

As fate brings these men together, the hunt for Eddie's son takes an unexpected turn for the worse, and they become embroiled in an inescapable and violent underworld of forced labour and modern slavery. As Eddie and Flynn fight to survive, each may find that the road to retribution starts within.

HIDDEN GRACE - A fast-paced, brutal and poignant tale about the dark recesses of human nature.

WITCHES COPSE

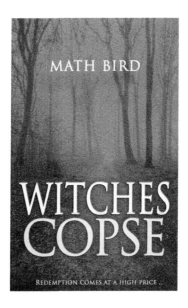

A gripping folk-horror occult-noir thriller in the tradition of *The Wicker Man, Kill List* and *The Witch*.

It's 1979, the Winter of Discontent, and gun for hire, Elizabeth Daton's career ends abruptly when a job results in a young girl being hospitalized. Her luck changes when renowned barrister Quentin Quinby hires her to travel to a remote Welsh village and escort an acquaintance of his back to London from the ominous Witches Copse.

Daton agrees, desperate to make amends, believing she's been given a second chance. But what begins as a simple errand quickly escalates into a terrifying ordeal of possession, witchcraft, and the occult.

Can Daton triumph, or is she doomed to pay redemption's price?

ACKNOWLEDGMENTS

The stories in this anthology first appeared as follows:

"Histories of the Dead" first published in *All Due Respect (7)*, 2015

"All the Hungry Ghosts" first published in *Plots with Guns*, 2014

"This Land of the Strange" first published in *Plan B Mystery Anthology (v)*, 2015

"The Darkness and the Light" first published in *Shotgun Honey*, 2013

"The Devilfish" first published in *Pulp Modern (9)*, 2015

"Your Father's Son" first published in *Shotgun Honey*, 2015

"Billy Star" first published in *Plots with Guns*, 2016

ABOUT THE AUTHOR

Math Bird is a British novelist and short story writer.

He's a member of the Crime Writers Association, and his work has aired on BBC Radio 4, Radio Wales, and Radio 4 Extra.

For more information:
www.mathbird.uk

Printed in Great Britain
by Amazon